Twice Goodbye

Darren John Wilson

First Edition Published in the United Kingdom
in 2025 by aSys Publishing

eBook Edition First Published in the United Kingdom
in 2025 by aSys Publishing

Disclaimer

This is a work of fiction. Names, characters, businesses, places, events and incidents are either the products of the author's imagination or used in a fictitious manner. Any resemblance to actual persons, living or dead, or actual events is purely coincidental.

ISBN: 978-1-913438-94-4
aSys Publishing 2025

Contents

ONE

Father

My father had a strange relationship with the truth. He always spoke the truth. That is what was strange about it. He did not know how to lie. Though much of what he said was as far removed from the truth as a peer of the realm is from the hovels of the dispossessed. He always *believed* that what he was saying was true. Therein lay his truth.

Drink was his nemesis. It ruined him and all that he touched. For him, one drink was not enough and two were too many. He was a decent man, always trying to do right by others, but nearly always doing wrong. He tried to stay sober but was nearly always drunk.

Drink had overseen the gradual dissipation of his career: from civil engineer to supermarket manager to neighbourhood odd-job man.

There was no "alcoholic gene" (that anyone knew of) in my father's family, and his upbringing had been idyllic. How the demon drink had taken hold of him, even three eminent psychologists had tried in vain to explain. There was no determinism with my father, no cause and effect, no reaction born of a particular action. There was only guesswork and speculation. Everything about him was nebulous, insubstantial. Touch him and you might have found yourself pushing at thin air. He might have been a ghost.

My father was a fantasist. That came to light when, shortly after my mother married him, she discovered that many of the salient details that he had given her about his childhood and adolescence were untrue. The problem (in terms of understanding what made him tick) was that the untruths that he had spoken about his past (and there were many) were, in every detail, so close to the truth that one wonders why he had ever seen the need to separate himself from it. So, to take but a sample of his minor deviations from the truth, instead of his having grown up on a Northumberland farm, he had spent his boyhood in a comfortable suburban home in genteel Durham; his parents had not been veterinarians (who had drifted into farming) but doctors; and, rather than having had a slightly younger sister, he had had a slightly older brother.

There were many other discrepancies of this type: small and insignificant in themselves, but large and significant enough, when put together, to suggest a man horribly ill at ease with himself and his person.

The details were interesting and suggestive of creativity at the heart of his being. The pattern, alas, was damning.

Why had he formulated these (apparently) inconsequential distortions of the truth? Had he been playing a game with himself and with us, his family? Or had some subtle unconscious psychic shift somehow occurred in his brain? To my mind, he was, indeed, a simple fantasist: unable (for reasons unknown even to himself) to manage the *actual* truth, he built around himself an *alternative* truth. He substituted one reality with another, and one that was not so different. It was as if he wanted to be a version of himself close enough to be recognisable, but different enough to be another body, another mind, into which he might slip, like a spare suit, whenever he needed a change.

He was too decent a man to lie. He had *no reason* to lie. He was too honourable a man to scheme at other people's expense. That is why I maintain that he was a fantasist. He was somehow mad. But he was not bad.

Had there been a relationship between my father's fantasist leanings and his drinking? There was correlation, perhaps, but causation is harder to show, harder still to prove. I have missed many a train, having left myself marooned on a station platform, momentarily transfixed, trying to fathom this bottomless mystery.

Was there any history of mental illness in my father's family? There was, I am sure, though show me the family where that is not the case.

What of suicide? What does his genealogy say about that? It is silent, for, as far as anyone knows, his family tree is not blighted by the sacrifice of self on the altar of personal despair.

Yet suicide is how my father met his end. He had picked a tree at random, it seems, amid Suffolk's rural pastures, and driven his car into it like the man possessed he must have been. Suicide was presumed because the balance of his mind had long been in doubt; the weather on the day he died had not been inclement; and no mechanical fault in his car had been detected.

The great irony about the crash was that my father had been supremely sober at the time. He had acted with reckless abandon at a time when reason and good sense should have restrained his impulse for self-destruction.

One act of madness and he was gone.

He was forty-one.

TWO

Mother

There is not much I can say about my mother. She was there; and then she was not. Cancer took her at the age of thirty-nine, two years before my father ploughed his car into the tree.

One often hears men described as "the strong silent type", yet virtually never women. My mother carried my father as a car carries a passenger: she conveyed him, and she gave him stability and direction, but without quite feeling the full weight of the burden. She was my father's humble servant, and she loved him. If she ever complained, nobody heard her. There was something joyful about her sacrifice, and I honour her as one who bore my father's weaknesses as if they were a blessing. She never uttered a word that she did not mean, and the words of her marriage vows, especially, were assuredly for keeps.

After her death, my father was like a ship without a rudder, or, indeed, a car without brakes, and some kind of collision with the world became inevitable.

They met amid a street party in full swing, during the summer of Her Majesty the Queen's Silver Jubilee year, when he had a mouth full of Victoria sponge cake and she was shooting a party blower at his face. Six months after that farcical introduction, they were married.

When I was a boy of nine, my father enjoined me never to marry for love, because (he said) love gets in the way of a perfectly serviceable relationship. "Marry a woman you *respect*," he urged me, "or even one you *admire*, but, if you ever find yourself *loving* a woman, do anything but marry her."

Well, my father was never one who felt obliged to live according to the principles he espoused: he duly succumbed to love and, had the drink not intervened, he would have yielded to happiness too.

My mother was never so complicated: she asked no questions of her vocation, knowing in her heart that it was simply her duty to love and to be loved.

For her, family was everything: she lived for it, and she might well have died for it too.

Might not her cancer have been brought on by her undoubted stoicism? Might she not have worn herself out with her relentless buttoned-up attention to duty?

About these matters—as with my father's inveterate fantasising and alcoholism, and any putative relationship between them—one can only speculate.

Intelligent people draw their own conclusions.

The upshot was that, by the age of ten, I was an orphan.

My brother, Irving, was thirteen.

THREE

Irving

Irving and I are not alone among siblings for being proximate rather than close: bound by ties of blood, we squat in the middle of each other's life like gargantuan toads and go through the motions of brotherhood like wheels turning in a clanking but well-oiled machine. The highs and lows of life are enjoyed and endured together, unavoidably so, but without highs and lows of fraternal feeling. I celebrate his successes, and he mine. When he needs a helping hand, I give it, and he does the same for me. Since my life (in adulthood, at least) has been more colourful than his, I have had more cause to lean on him than he has on me. He has always been a redoubt, something strong and solid upon which to lean, so much so that he shames me with his unbending dependability.

Irving is so resilient that I often wonder if he is entirely human, as if he might be in possession of some alien DNA. He came through our troubled childhood without so much as a scratch. If anyone could be dragged through a hedge backwards and emerge unscathed, it is Irving. Nothing fazes him. He is unwavering. At eighteen, he joined a firm of accountants, qualified with indecent haste (as a chartered accountant), and then became an absurdly young partner in the company. A minimum of fuss would be too much for him. He is unflappable. He could diffuse a bomb, blindfold, without so much as a flinch, and, if the bomb were to go off, he would not be moved, and the shrapnel would bounce off him. If he is never calm in a crisis, it is only because, with him, there is never even the hint of a crisis, only a situation to be managed.

The claret once ran out in his wine cellar. That, for him, was a crisis, but he came through the disaster with commendable fortitude.

His daughter recently went up to Edinburgh University to study medicine, having missed out on a place at Oxford by the very narrowest of margins. The girl had been inconsolable, crestfallen at having let down the family. All Irving had been able to say on the matter was: "It's unfortunate."

A nuclear conflagration for Irving would be "regrettable".

Though I consider myself a phlegmatic character, I am a corybantic ecstatic prophet, compared with Irving, or one of the Romantic poets on acid.

I do not criticise my brother, only comment on who he is.

If I were to submit any charge by way of criticism, it would be that he has an irritating tendency to treat me like a schoolboy. This obnoxious trait of his came to the fore on the Sunday after I informed him that I planned to risk my marriage (as he saw it) by going in pursuit of an old flame (as he called the woman in question).

His schoolmasterly demeanour follows from his fundamental straightness, against which he defines my crookedness (as he sees it). My brother is so straight that there is not the slightest hint of a kink or a curve in his makeup. He is a human ruler with an inbuilt slide-rule of bourgeois values that defy his discomforting start in life.

So it was that he sat with me at the bar of the Mill Hotel, in Sudbury, on that Sunday lunchtime, beer in hand, holding forth and taking me to task with enough self-righteous moral authority to shame the Dalai Lama and the Pope combined.

On the day before, I had finally made the decision which provoked Irving's indignation. It was not a crisis since, as we have seen, Irving does not do crises; it was more a case of my having affronted his sense of propriety and decency; of my having (again) put myself in a situation profoundly alien to his moral sensibility.

Irving and I had once discussed morality. He had told me that he recoiled from the word "immoral" since he possessed no moral code by which he might evaluate human conduct. His morality derives from a sense of order based upon numbers and how they are arranged into columns of credit (good) and debit (bad).

His trade is inextricably bound up with his values.

When he pronounces judgement, it is the accountant speaking.

FOUR

Brotherhood

It was a simple road sign that prompted me to embark on the venture that Irving saw as pure folly. In Sudbury, there had been a campaign going on for some time to restrict the speed limit to twenty miles per hour in residential areas. The sign read: "Twenty Is Plenty." That word, "twenty", was the trigger, the firing of the gun, which had launched me from the starting blocks at which I had long been poised. I had known for years that I would go in search of Leanne. The urge to do so had been growing inside me, stalking my being like a quiet but determined predator. I had been looking over my shoulder at something I could barely see, yet knowing it was there; until it caught up with me, and overtook me, demanding that I follow in its wake.

Mawkishness, sadness and nostalgia: these are all sentiments to which I consider myself immune, as much a stranger to my consciousness as a duchess is to a roadside café. These three reprobates, then, are not the reasons why I became resolved to take up my memory of Leanne and go with it in search of Leanne herself.

My wife Donna, naturally, was the first person to hear of my plans; she gave them her blessing with no apparent reservation, though I could tell that she was hurting inside, as if the mutual trust built upon fifteen years of marriage had been stabbed at with a blunt knife.

There had been no guarantee that she would give her blessing to my intended archaeological mission to excavate the past. She was not the Virgin Mary at the Annunciation, and I was not the angel Gabriel inviting her to conform herself to the Divine Will. She was the wife of a man taking liberties with his marriage, and she had every right to ask him to think again.

As it turned out, Donna *had* been the Virgin Mary to my angel Gabriel; she had been full of grace (of the human sort); she had not so much bent to my will as cooperated with it.

Predictably, as we chatted over a beer on that Sunday, Irving was not slow in reminding me of my responsibilities to my wife. I had known what his attitude would be, and the exact words that he had used in admonishing me had not been hard to predict. He shook his head so many times during the interview that his neck must still be aching as I write. Had I told him that I was thinking of circumnavigating the Sahara Desert on a skateboard, he would have shaken his head in the same condescending manner.

"Saturday, August the sixth, two-thousand-and-twenty-two," he began.

"What about it?"

"Mark that as the day you threw away fifteen years of marriage."

I reminded Irving that I had told Donna what I was planning to do, and that she had raised no objection.

"No *apparent* objection," he replied.

I sighed wearily and braced myself for the interrogation to come. We were two men of one blood, and with a common experience, but with temperaments different enough to clash whenever life's vicissitudes conspired to put the interests of the one at odds with those of the other.

What *were* my interests in the matter at hand, and what were his?

Mine were simply rooted in benign selfishness, for I was merely curious to know whether Leanne were still alive. There was a somewhat deeper yearning, too, of course, but it was the urge to satisfy my curiosity that was directing me, prompting me, and pointing the way to Fleetpool, that run-down northern seaside town where, for just one year, I had been blissfully happy.

Irving's response to my revelation was governed by his sense of reason and proportion; as we have seen, he is a supremely upright man, and that uprightness is born of a quiet determination to protect himself from a past that always threatens to intrude on his future. His entire psychological and physiological constitution is a kind of dam, keeping the past at bay, the past being vast waters with the power to break through at any moment, without warning, to overwhelm him and the chess-piece orderliness of a life arranged with a military-style attention to detail.

At every turn in our discussion, I saw where Irving was coming from, and I acknowledged his every point (made in his typically pompous and self-righteous manner) graciously, though without so much as considering changing the path

I had chosen. Such was the pattern of our communication. My brother is as straight as a hatstand, and often twice as ridiculous, and it is my habit to use him as a sounding board, listening to his voice of impeccable reason whilst remaining steadfast in my resolve to do whatever I have determined to do.

I once lost money on an investment, an amount that was not insignificant, and before committing the money had consulted Irving on the wisdom of backing the scheme in question. He had warned me in no uncertain terms against it.

There were times, then, when I had cause to regret disregarding his advice.

He had counselled caution when I married Donna. She herself was not the reason for his wish that I should think twice before taking the marital plunge, but, rather, where, through her, I would find myself living and working. He had questioned the wisdom of my marrying a publican.

I had asked him to elucidate, and he had answered that working in a pub would stifle my creativity: it would stymie my art. He had never cared much for my art before, seeing it as little more than a romantic sideshow in my life, so his sudden concern for the future of my artistic vocation was touching.

He had then asked if I thought it wise for me to live in a pub, what with our paternal heritage and all, and I had told him not to be so ridiculous.

"Just be careful," he had replied, "that's all I'm saying."

Irving and reason are good together, they fit each other like hand and glove, but they were horribly mismatched on that occasion.

Again and again, as we talked on that Sunday, Irving screwed up his face in the agony of thought, appearing to reflect on the lost cause that I am, and he drank beer, thirstily, as if his very sanity depended upon it.

Irving told me that, up to a point, he understood where I was coming from, that he appreciated that the year I had spent in that "depressing" northern town was the happiest time of my life, adding, with a touch of spite, that all that belonged in the past. I buried it twenty years ago, he declared, and now I wanted to go rummaging around in the graveyard. He was sure that I did not need to know whether Leanne were alive or dead, and he wondered, given that Leanne lived life on the edge, what were the chances that she *were* alive. At my claim that I *sensed* that she was very much alive, he scoffed, and he was silent when I asked him if he had never sensed something before. Rousseau said that we feel before we think. Irving, I suspect, is the exception that proves that rule. I was carrying a torch for Leanne, Irving continued, but I needed to let her go. I protested that I had been letting her go for twenty years, that I had not heard from her during that time, and he was forthright in declaiming that that was even more reason to let her go.

Only once during our meeting in the Mill Hotel, on that first Sunday in August, did rancour threaten to intrude and overtake us, and that threat came when Irving reminded me that Leanne had nearly cost me my life.

"I had to save Leanne," I retorted. "Should I have let her drown?"

"I don't care about Leanne."

"Well, you should."

"Why should I?"

"Because *I* care about her."

"What is she to me?"

"She's whatever you want her to be, which, apparently, is nothing at all."

"I tell you who I *do* care about. I care about your wife. I care about what your going after this girl will do to Donna."

I noticed that he had left me out. But I let that go. I had long ago noticed his affection for my wife. But I let that go too.

That was the cue for me to invoke again that number, twenty, or, to be precise, twice twenty, which is forty, the age that both Leanne and I would reach on the fifteenth day of that month.

That, indeed, was the crux of the matter.

Leanne and I had parted at the age of twenty and we were now approaching forty. A few months before, the word, "forty", had been whispering in my ear; as time passed, the whisper had become louder and louder, like a gathering storm rumbling in the distance; now it was bellowing at me, and from close range, so that it was all I could do not to be deafened by the power of its scream.

The chasm between my thinking and Irving's was thereby exposed. The questions and assertions from Irving duly came thicker and faster. He was on a roll, more inquisitive lawyer now than plodding accountant.

My answers were those of a hapless defendant in court trying to weather the cross-examination.

"Why can't you just look her up online? *She* could have looked *you* up. Is it not the case that Leanne has never bothered looking for you; that she's never even *thought* about looking for you; that she's simply left you in the distant past, where you belong, and where she belongs for you?"

"Where is the romance in looking someone up online? In any case, I *have* looked up Leanne online, but there's no trace of her. Yes, she might have looked me up, but I don't use social media and, the pub aside, my online footprint is negligible."

"Romance? You're a married man, Frankie!"

"I've squared it with Donna."

"Leanne could be anywhere: Australia, say, or South Africa, or Walnut Creek, California."

"Again, I *sense* that Leanne is in Fleetpool, or thereabouts."

"What do you plan to do: knock on every door in the north-west of England?"

"If I seek out the people I knew up there, and ask them enough questions, then, eventually, I'll find Leanne."

"People will have moved on. You're hardly likely to find the place exactly as it was, twenty years on, are you?"

"There will be enough up there for me to work with."

"Were you in love with Leanne?"

"What is love?"

"There's no need to go philosophical on me, Frankie. I know you've read a lot of books these past ten years or so, and been to night school, but I'm a humble accountant, I see things in black and white, in columns and rows of figures, in terms of debit and credit."

"Whatever my feelings were for Leanne back then, they haven't changed."

Wittgenstein said that most of the problems that blight human life, however big or small, can be attributed to poor communication: people, he said, are simply too careless about, and imprecise in, what they say, using words unthinkingly, neither knowing nor caring what they really mean.

Though Irving and I came at each other from opposite directions, we factored that into our communication: we knew that we were different, and we made allowances for our difference.

Thus was I able to laugh at his false modesty when he described himself as a humble accountant: when he spoke in this way, he was not claiming humility, he was asserting the supremacy of the creed by which he lived and worked.

Moreover, I had to chuckle at his "night school" jibe. That is what he called gaining a degree in philosophy from the Open University? That was another one for me to let go.

Our discussions invariably ended in silence on his part. Irving understood me but, at the same time, he was perplexed by my type. As we finished drinking our second pints of ale, he had never looked more perplexed. He looked like a man standing in the middle of the desert without a compass, not knowing which way to turn.

When I told him that I was leaving Sudbury for Fleetpool, at ten o'clock the following morning, he looked more than perplexed, he looked mortified, like a man condemned to spending the rest of his life labouring over an insoluble puzzle.

FIVE

Place

A place is much like a person for having both a body and a soul: the body of a place is its very fabric, the stuff of which it is made; and its soul is its *genius loci*, or the spirit which animates it, and which endows it with essential being.

Each one of us has a soul, but it takes a person *of* soul to intuit the soul of a place which is its essence; and that essence is no subjective thing, but a thing unchangeable, and a thing unchanged since its very fusion with the created body in a moment of time.

Divining this eternal principle in a place is no act of will, it is the expression of a sensibility given to but few; that sensibility, indeed, is a gift of discernment which is tantamount to a calling, and one for which few are chosen.

A place given spirit by *genius loci* can be a thing of nature, a windswept mountainside, perhaps, or a shimmering lake, or a deserted beach. Literature abounds with such otherworldly temples of nature—and the spirits which move them are not necessarily benignant—places so hallowed as to be sanctuaries for those with the gift of perception: one thinks of E. M. Forster's dell at Madingley, in *The Longest Journey*; or Joan Lindsay's Hanging Rock; or the Mount Tabor of scripture, the essence of which immense natural beauty drew the very event, Christ's Transfiguration, which guaranteed its place beyond mortality.

Something put together by human hands is no less entitled than a thing of nature to be haunted by *genius loci*, and it need not be a relic of Classical Antiquity to qualify, or a famous landmark of a renowned city; it can be a disused warehouse in Bolton, or a municipal housing estate in Cowdenbeath.

There are places, many of them, devoid of this spirit of animation. A place so unmoved is barren and we might call it a desolation. It gives out nothing and from it we receive nothing. It is inert, and so are we in response to it.

Fleetpool, for all its tackiness and vulgarity, is emphatically not such a place.

SIX

Return

Return to a place after an absence of twenty years and we would expect that place to have changed, if only superficially, and that any changes would be instantly recognisable, in the same way that we would be struck by someone's ageing had we not set eyes on them for two decades.

The tone was set as soon as I drove into Fleetpool through the town's easternmost suburb, Berkely, and beheld the same familiar signpost proclaiming Fleetpool to be the suntrap of the north and announcing it as the town that has been twinned with Paderborn, in Austria, since 1975. The signpost had lost much of its sheen, and it looked rather tatty and jaded, much, I suspected, as I would find the town itself.

As I drove along the seafront, past the lighthouse and the war memorial, I saw nothing new, though I knew that I was only minutes away from encountering something that would strike me as having changed almost beyond recognition.

I speak of what had been my home, on and off during my previous sojourn in Fleetpool, the Marine Gardens Guest

House, then owned and run by a Mrs Gwendoline Baxter, but now the Marine Gardens Hotel, owned by the Inverdale Group of Hotels & Leisure. I had booked mine and Leanne's old room, number six, and the photographs on the hotel's website had given me some idea of what to expect in terms of outward changes.

The scene that greeted me upon my arrival, however, was still a shock.

In its conversion from guesthouse to hotel, my erstwhile home had been smartened and enlarged. Gone was the pocked stucco and the peeling paint, and no more was the rundown and uninviting exterior. The place was aglow in brilliant white, almost transfigured compared with its former drab shabbiness, and neither the building itself, with its size-able new annexe, nor the surrounding gardens was any the less resplendent for being rained upon by a dismal sky.

There were puddles aplenty between the carpark and the spectacular entrance to the revamped building, all of them shallow little lakes and so numerous that there was little point in walking around them.

My overriding impression as I stood at the threshold of the hotel and looked around, and across the road at the seafront, was that the place seemed at once familiar and unreal, as though I were revisiting a fantasy for the umpteenth time, an ever-unfolding mental story that I knew better than I knew my own life, whilst knowing that it was nothing more than a waking dream.

That experience was entirely subjective: my mind was simply adjusting to being back in a place that had for me acquired an almost mystical significance, as I struggled to reconcile the old with the new.

Inside, the foyer had been transformed: the old burgundy carpet was gone, and in its place were squares of corporate blue; at the reception desk, instead of Mrs Baxter trilling away like a deranged canary to the secretary working in the back room, was a young lady in a royal-blue outfit who greeted me with a fixed smile and eyes that were in Fleetpool but wishing they were in the Seychelles. The receptionist was standing at her post like someone at a launderette waiting for her washing to finish. I had seen more animation in a chess master deep in concentration and plotting his next move.

She wished me a good afternoon as if she were addressing a headstone in a graveyard.

Whereas I did not feel quite like a headstone, I had been made to feel like a shrunken garment just emerging from her washing-machine.

Spun-dry and diminished, I greeted her in return.

I could see from the Inverdale Group badge pinned on her jacket lapel that her name was Nadine, and I wondered if I had ever known anyone of that name. A Nadia, definitely, but I could recall no Nadine.

"I used to stay here when it was a humble guest house," I said, trying to inject some bonhomie into our fledgeling relationship.

Nadine nodded as if I had just said something with which she agreed, though already I knew enough about her to suspect that she would have trouble agreeing with anyone about anything.

Of all the characters that I encountered in Fleetpool—and elsewhere, for my inquiries would take me to several other places in the north of England, on both the west coast and the east—during my eight-day stay, Nadine was the most interesting, if only because for one so young she had a precocious sense of self and where she wanted to go in life, together with an adorable lack of affectation; unlike most of the other people that I came across, in those few days, she was one whose life was ahead of her, and she was full of the optimism and bravado of youth, with none of the jaded cynicism and smouldering regrets of her elders.

We became such good friends, courtesy of our regular chats as I passed reception, on my way out and on my way back in, that, when I took my leave of Fleetpool, on the evening of Monday the fifteenth, I gave her a lift to Norwich, where she would stay with an auntie before embarking on her new life.

"The place was a proper dive before Inverdale bought it, a right fleapit," Nadine said. "It was run by some old dear called Gwendoline Baxter."

"Mrs Baxter was not that old," I said. Leanne and I had seen her as someone too old to be our mother, but too young to be our grandmother, which made her old *now*, and there was I hoping that she was still in the land of the living, since I was planning to begin tracking her down in the morning.

"When you're twenty-two, like me, even thirty's old, isn't it?"

"Do you happen to know where Mrs Baxter went after she left here?"

"No idea, though you could check the municipal cemetery."

This Nadine was a receptionist with a difference and, despite her irreverence—*because* of it, I dare say—I found her strangely refreshing.

"It's a wet Monday afternoon in Fleetpool," I said. "I'm depressed enough."

Nadine treated me to a smile that was as warm and genuine as my late maternal grandparents' fireplace, which had lent their old cottage in Long Melford a modicum of cosiness in an otherwise grim and cheerless dwelling. Her teeth were so white and perfect that I wondered if she might not be afraid to eat and drink in case she spoilt them. I would have been had I possessed teeth even half as good as hers.

"I'm Frankie McDowell," I said.

Nadine checked the register quickly and then gave me the key to room six. She did not need to know my history with room six, no more than I needed to know what Nadine told me next.

"There was a couple in room six last week, on their honeymoon. Can you imagine it? Honeymooning in Fleetpool? Anyway, they were at it like rabbits the whole week, day and night. Several people staying here complained about the noise, one of them some old bat with a broken hearing aid, who *still* heard them, they were *that* loud. An office worker in the building next door complained. Some people out on the street complained."

I had to laugh. "Should you be telling me all this?"

"It's no skin off my nose," Nadine replied. "I'm out of here on Friday."

"Have you got a new job?"

"New *job*? New *life*, more like. I'm going to Australia to work for my uncle. He owns a hotel in Sydney."

"Well," I said, "the Australians are bound to fall in love with your boundless English charm."

SEVEN

Rooms

As we go through life, we collect rooms like we collect people, though for most of us the people outnumber the rooms. What kind of rooms might we collect? Childhood bedrooms, classrooms, honeymoon suites, offices, grandparents' living-rooms (with their evocations of another age), and marital bedrooms: these are the types of rooms that shape our lives and enrich our memories, for the better, we hope, rather than the worse.

We might collect between five and ten such rooms: any more and we might perhaps have lived too itinerant a life.

Room six of the Marine Gardens Guest House (as I prefer to remember it), in Fleetpool, is one of my six or seven collectable rooms. It is not just my room. It is Leanne's too. It is *our* room.

It had been a twin room in our day but was now a double.

The room was substantially the same. It was *essentially* the same. Its shape and dimensions were unaltered. Its fabric was as fixed and as solid as before. The colours of the walls had changed, and old furniture had been replaced by new.

I sensed Leanne's presence. I could hear her soft voice and gentle laugh. I could see her moving around and between the beds, as well as her resting her elbows on the windowsill as she looked down on the street below, and her going into the bathroom and her coming out, always cheerful and content, despite her precarious hold on life. She was always bashing her shins on the edges and corners of the beds, and then shrieking in pain, so that her legs were always battered and bruised, bloodied, and covered in scabs. I used to tell her to look where she was going, and she would reply that there was "not enough room to swing a rat in this pokey little place". She was not ungrateful, for she cherished Mrs Baxter and her kindness (for letting us use room six whenever we wanted or needed it, though I had offered time after time to pay). Leanne was inveterately clumsy, and she knew it. If she were in a room the size of Switzerland, furnished by a single chair, she would trip over that chair, or walk into it, several times a day. She had once stumbled into the grandfather clock on the first-floor landing and complained, as she nursed her stubbed toe and bruised forehead, that it was "a bloody stupid place to put a clock". Now, as I listened to the hush of the room, I heard her voice again, and I knew that, somehow and somewhere, she was close to me.

Where was Donna at that moment? What was she doing? Did I really care?

I sent her a text message, asking her how she was and letting her know that I had arrived, but without much feeling, almost absently, as though the connection between us had been severed.

Leanne and I were back in our room, and I had yet to meet Donna.

My love was out there, close enough for me to reach out and touch her.

I would go out and find her.

EIGHT

Agency

I thank my Uncle Brian and Auntie Anne for making of both me and my brother men in something approaching full control of our respective destinies; men able to navigate our way through life making sensible decisions; men capable of taking responsibility for what we do and for the consequences of what we do.

Seeing their nephews, Irving and Frankie, orphaned as boys, with adulthood a long way in the future, it would have been all too easy to let them be taken into care. Brian and Anne Elliott, however, were better people than that. The word "great" is used almost always to describe public figures—statesmen, artists, scientists, and such like—and yet it is the "little" people performing "little" acts of charity and kindness that are the true greats, for, without them and their beneficence, there would be no stage for the "big" people from which to project their greatness. It is the likes of Brian and Anne who make the world go round, and who avert crisis after crisis with their steadfastness and integrity, and with their sense of honour and duty.

If the talented of this world do what they can, and the geniuses do what they must, people like Brian and Anne, possessing neither talent nor genius, can do only what is right and just, obeying the spontaneous promptings of their hearts.

Irving and I are the men we are because of who Brian and Anne were and are. I feel no shame in saying so, no sense of our having been remiss in the shaping and moulding of our own persons, because, at the ages of thirteen and ten, respectively, Irving and I were effectively at their mercy, relying on them to save us from the children's home, a place that would have changed us irrevocably for the worse. They steadied our ship, they set it on a course, and they gave us the tools to keep it on course and to take it where we would.

I was only eighteen when I left the home (and the care) of Brian and Anne Elliott (Anne is my mother's sister) to go and live in Southwold, a gorgeous little town on the beautiful Suffolk coast; and I was able to leave at such a tender age, confident that I knew what I was doing, because of who my uncle and auntie had helped me become.

One day—I had just turned eighteen—I was in a café, in Sudbury, sketching, trying my hand at a spot of art, curious to see what emerged on the sketchpad, when a man of about thirty took it upon himself to park himself at my table and begin expounding on my evident (to him) potential as an artist.

Within a week, I was living in his big house by the sea, being taught the rudiments of painting with oils and acrylic. His name was Marcel. He had established a community of artists in the house bought for him by his parents, five years previously, upon their decision to move to California to seek a life with more sea, sand and sunshine than even the sandy and sunny seaside Southwold was able to offer.

In addition to Marcel and me, there were four other artists (with others coming and going) living in ramshackle but productive harmony, churning out commonplace pictures of local scenery for credulous local punters. Marcel used to call us "painters for punters", though I suspect that he was hoping that we would graduate to serious art, having mastered the techniques of the trade in the vulgar pursuit of profit. Marcel knew the local market inside out, which enabled each member of the group—the most unlikely colony of creatives the world will ever see—to bask in a wholly unexpected prosperity.

I saw that initial period of my life as an artist—my Southwold Period—as an opportunity to develop and hone my technique: the more personal (and abstract) works (I knew) would come later.

As it transpired, Southwold was the ideal place for me to serve my artistic apprenticeship for being free of any bohemian influences that might have taken my work in a prematurely pretentious direction; its simple, uncomplicated beauty provided the perfect setting for an extended tutorial in the science of art.

Nearly a year after my career as an artist had begun in earnest, Marcel took me aside and gave me a fatherly talk about the perils of resting on my artistic laurels.

"Leave," he urged me. "Get out of your comfort zone."

On hearing this rather alarming injunction, my first thought was that he was trying to oust me to make room in the house for a new protégé, but he happened to be serious. He practically ordered me to go to Fleetpool, a place he had chosen some years before for having nothing in common with Southwold apart from the sea. Fleetpool, he said, had made him as an artist, and he was confident that it would do the same for me.

I trusted him implicitly. After all, how could a man who had all the answers to questions I had not even asked possibly be wrong?

That is how my association with Fleetpool began.

That is why, a few days into my twentieth year, on a warm August Bank Holiday Monday, I arrived in Fleetpool with little more than the clothes on my back, a few pencils and brushes, and a sketchbook.

Marcel had told me about the shop in the town where I could buy materials for my painting.

There would not be a Fleetpool Period in my career, a few sketches aside, for not a drop of oil from my hand would touch canvas during my twelve-month stay in the north-west. Years later, there were paintings inspired by the memory of my time in Fleetpool, but at the time productivity eluded me as an eel escapes the grip of a human hand.

One of those paintings was in the boot of my car, boxed and elaborately padded for protection.

If I found Leanne, she would see it.

It would blow her mind.

NINE

Exploration

David Livingstone, who famously ranged over and traversed the central African watershed in search of the source of the Nile River, and Granny Smith, shuffling among the shelves of her local supermarket, have at least one thing in common: both are explorers.

We all explore.

We explore all the time: all day and every day; for the most part in pursuit of the most mundane tasks, but often in connection with undertakings of a more audacious kind, where a certain boldness and vigour is needed in response to the inner voice calling us to investigate or to search out.

That, indeed, is the meaning of the verb "to explore": to investigate or search out.

We explore places.

We explore time whenever we remember.

We explore ourselves. When we do so, we explore both time and place.

We explore when we embark on (what one of my philosophy professors once rather grandiosely termed) "the thrill of the academic chase".

To explore is to venture into the unknown; or to delve more deeply into what we know already, to gain a new understanding, perhaps; or to reacquaint ourselves with the familiar.

We are bound to explore.

Unlike the animals, we are not driven to explore by instinct alone. We explore for the sake of edification. We explore for the sake of love.

My first stay in Fleetpool was an exercise in wide-eyed youthful observation of all things new, living life forwards, and at great pace, not stopping to review the little that was past in search of understanding; my second visit to the town would be a matter of plodding ahead whilst endeavouring to make sense of the expanse of time that lay behind me and that had caused me, with not inconsiderable impertinence, to put my life on hold.

During this trip, the new would visit me but it would interest me only insofar as it impinged on the old. There was so much to discover, so much to uncover, even as I took in sights and sounds and smells that could not have been more familiar. In the old was the new concealed, and in the new would the old be revealed. That was my hope. That was my conviction.

As I stepped out onto the street, at about four-thirty on the first Monday of my stay (there would be no second Tuesday or any other second day of the week), I felt as though my investigation were properly under way. I was the private detective working for himself, with no client paying me except the passage of time and the consolations of increased wisdom that came with it.

I wandered over to the tacky little café opposite the pier and adjacent to the Dome cinema; in mine and Leanne's day, it had traded as Eric's Diner but now offered itself to the world as Peter's Pans. The Eric Catterick I knew was not the type of man to inject seaside humour into the title of his business, but as such he never left himself vulnerable to having his sense of humour panned.

As I drank my tea, staring out at the rain and the streets that glistened in the light given by the sun trying to peep through the grey-black blanket of cloud, which caused little prisms of colour to shimmer in the puddles, I reflected that Leanne and I might just, by some visitation of freakish good luck, simply chance upon each other. Might she not breeze into the café, any moment now, and stare at me, aghast, as she beheld the ghost from her dim and distant past? Might I not step out of the café, in ten minutes' time, and walk straight into her? There was no doubt in my mind that we would recognise each other, even after so long and with the masks of age covering our faces.

"Walk past the café now, Leanne," I said to myself, though the lady sitting at the table next to mine thought I was addressing the window. "Walk past the window. Save me the trouble of looking for you. Give us one more week together—one more *day* even—before we part forever. You want that, don't you? Let the Providence that brought us together bring us together one last time." The lady at the neighbouring table shifted uneasily in her seat, unsure (I guessed) whether to dismiss me as a lunatic or report me to the police.

The clouds dispersed and the sun came out as if it intended to stay out for long enough for people to enjoy it; and out people came from their hiding places, like ants spilling out of a nest, blindly heeding some call of nature. They poured onto the promenade, onto the beach, and even into the sea, and I marvelled at the dedication of people to the idea that the seaside in England in August is a pleasant place to be as long as the sun is shining and the wind not quite strong enough to blow one off one's feet.

Though my plans for the days ahead were tentative, ideas about how to go about looking for Leanne were becoming more solid in my mind; a framework, at least, was starting to take shape.

On the first afternoon and evening of my visit, I would simply drift around town, taking in the atmosphere, feeding on memories, waiting for inspiration to guide me.

Even as I floated in this most insubstantial of mental clouds, I was certain that I would soon be thanking Providence for matching me with its hour.

For a while, I sat on a bench on the promenade and observed the people on the beach. They looked like the same people that I had got used to seeing twenty years before: the same families, the same parents, the same children, the same clothes, outfits and swimwear.

Even on such a dismal day, vibrant colours abounded, and this incongruous chromatic flamboyance was accentuated by the saris dotted across the pebbles and wet sand.

The tide was in but going out.

I watched as two children (they had to be brother and sister) fought over a beachball, just as I had seen them in the past, and I recalled even the baritone admonishment of the father, and the shrieking intervention of the mother, as auditory replicas from another time.

"Give me my ball back, you cow!"

"Don't call me a cow, you pig!"

"If you two don't stop fighting, I'll bang your heads together!"

"She started it!"

"He did!"

"One more word from you two and we're going home!"

"It's not fair!"

"Shut it!"

After that little performance, I shook my head in amusement and sauntered over to the pier. To my surprise, there was a turnstile at the entrance, and I had to pay a pound to get past it. The pleasure of walking on unstable planks of wood, with large gaps between them, whilst doing one's best not to be blown overboard, used to be free.

It was nowhere near warm enough for something cold and refreshing, but the teenaged girl in the little sweetshop by the amusement arcade looked so crushed by listlessness that I felt compelled to keep her on her toes by purchasing an ice-cream incorporating a chocolate flake. I was given the ice-cream without the flake. It could have been worse. I could have been given the flake without the ice-cream. I might just have complained about that.

When I reached the end of the pier, more memories drifted into my mind like the clouds floating across the prospect. There we were, Leanne and I, our nineteen-year-old selves, standing beside me, lowering a large bucket attached to a rope into the sea, and then pulling it back up filled with seaweed and crabs.

We always returned the creatures to the water, alive, but one day we caught a crustacean so large that I suggested we take it back to the guest house for Mrs Baxter to cook for our dinner.

Snippets of dialogue came back to me.

"We're taking it nowhere. We're putting it back where it came from."

"Why?"

"How would you like to be boiled alive?"

"It's just a crab, Leanne."

"And you're a human being. You're better than a crab. So *be* better than a crab."

Leanne had often given me food for thought with her quaint little sayings, and I cherished them now as the tokens of endearment that they were.

The sky had darkened again, and the wind was getting angry, so I retreated to a shelter to put the wind at my back. The ice-cream was long devoured, and I was becoming hungry for something more nutritious, which ruled out the candyfloss and toffee apples on offer at the stall to my left. Reckoning on a pretentiously expensive menu back at the hotel, I decided to have dinner at the Queen's Arms. Leanne and I had often amused ourselves there with food and drink, and the company of some of the locals with their oblique views on life and homespun wisdom.

I reckoned with the continued proprietorship of Angela Palmer, for she had been only in her forties when Leanne and I were frequenting the pub, and I hoped that she and the punters between them would have an inkling of what had happened to Leanne after the harrowing events of the August Bank Holiday of twenty years ago.

I moved along the beach to the spot where Leanne and I used to watch Jack fishing. Jack was a kindly old man who would pluck fish from the sea with consummate ease and take them home for his tea. He used to maintain that there was a skill to what he did, when it seemed to Leanne and me that his sport consisted of little more than pointing a rod at the sea and waiting for the unsuspecting fish to bite.

We had expected to hear tales of himself as a young man on fishing expeditions in exotic locations—the Caribbean, perhaps, or the South Sea Islands—but he assured us that the only time he had ever ventured outside Fleetpool had been to serve in the Royal Lancashire Fusiliers, 2nd Battalion, in World War Two, when he had seen action at Dunkirk and then later in Tunisia, Sicily, and mainland Italy.

He told us that he had "dodged a few bullets" in his time, and that the war had educated him in many ways, but that it was an education that he could have done without, all things considered.

"Jack has fished his last," I said to myself as I gazed out at the horizon, "and must now be fishing in some Elysian waters to his heart's content."

If Jack were still alive then he was as old as the hills and about as mobile.

The spot where Jack fished was the same spot where Leanne and I had been forced to retrieve our clothes after a sudden gust of wind had blown them down the beach when we were bathing naked in the sea one night down by the pier.

I laughed at the memory.

The bandstand was still there, I noticed as I crossed Beach House Park, and I felt reassured by the affirmation that something as quaint as a bandstand hosting brass bands playing catchy tunes in English seaside towns still existed in the harsh, unsentimental climate of the modern world.

The bandstand held a special place in my heart, notwithstanding the fact that the night I had spent sleeping in it was singularly the most uncomfortable of my life. It was dripping with rain as I beheld it now, but my memory of it was as clear as the sky had been on those first few August days and nights after my arrival twenty-one years before. Hours after Leanne and I first met, she had persuaded me to spend the night with her in her makeshift home. We had slept sitting with our backs against the inner wall of the bandstand, huddled together, using our jackets as blankets and our bags as pillows, and had awoken (from what little sleep we had managed to get) to the sight of a middle-aged lady looking down at us, curiously, from what had seemed to be a great height, and a black Labrador puppy sniffing at our persons, with the same curiosity, as it interrogated us for evidence of life.

On subsequent days, I toured all the other places where Leanne and I had whiled away many a frivolous hour, and my tour included visits to Gary, Larry and Brenda.

Who were these strange people?

They were not people, they were, indeed, places.

Gary was the golf course, the crazy golf course. Larry was the lighthouse. Brenda was the beach hut. Leanne liked to personalise things and places in that way. Gordon was the guest house. Bob was the bandstand. Peter was the pier. Her tendency to anthropomorphise might have been a subconscious throwback to her childhood, a time of life when animals and vehicles talk, and fairy tales seem more real than life itself.

There were times when Leanne and I had been so bent on having fun that we would scrounge money and use it to pay for a few rounds of crazy golf, rather than spend it on food and drink. We had occupied many hours trying to feed golf balls into and round miniature castles, over miniature bridges, and through miniature tunnels. She always came out of herself, no matter how low her mood, when we were playing crazy golf. Her inner child would come out, leaping and bounding, an exuberant, effervescent bundle of irrepressible energy.

As for the lighthouse, there was great irony there, for the keeper's name was, indeed, Larry. One winter's afternoon, Leanne had persuaded Larry to take us on an impromptu tour of the lighthouse. He had taken us to the top of the edifice, from which vantage point we were treated to a panoramic view of the sea and the town and its surroundings. My fear of heights had taken me down the spiralling concrete steps much quicker than I had ascended them, and from the safety of the promenade had waited for Leanne, and waited, and waited some more, until, after about an hour, she emerged so wildly enthused by what Larry had shown her of the inner workings of the lighthouse that she vowed to become a lighthouse-keeper once she had got her head into some sort of order.

It occurred to me, then, as I drifted around the town with no apparent purpose, that I should be looking for Leanne at what she might now be calling Leanne the lighthouse, successor to Larry.

The idea was too fanciful to entertain.

"Our" beach hut was still there (at any rate, there was a beach hut on the spot where "our" beach hut had been). It had become our beach hut one April evening, when Leanne had seized upon the loose-fitting lock on the door and, with minimal force and a startling sleight-of-hand, enticed it open with a hairpin. Leanne would use the same hairpin to open and close the lock at will, at intervals, whenever we needed nightly shelter from the elements. Inside, there had not been much in the way of creature comforts, but it had given us a roof over our heads at those times when Leanne's mind went absent without leave and she was eschewing the sanctuary afforded by the guest house. We had given up our cramped little refuge when the owners returned to use it during the summer months and had taken care to leave it exactly as we had found it.

The Pavilion Ballroom was a bulbous construction at the base of the pier. It remained a ballroom, I was delighted to see, still hosting, as I noticed with a glance at the posters promoting future events, the Seniors' Ballroom Dance, on Tuesday afternoons, at three o'clock. Leanne and I had often insinuated ourselves into the Seniors' Ballroom Dance and pilfered any food and drink lying around to be pilfered, not put off by the pervasive aroma of incontinence and antiseptic, a heady mixture of clinic and public convenience.

If the word "seniors" described people of retirement age then the folk that Leanne and I had seen shuffling around the Pavilion Ballroom dancefloor were a decade or two past the threshold of retirement—retirement-age-plus, one might say—positively geriatric as they were, men and women who might well have been able to recall the launching of the Titanic and identify it with their childhood.

Leanne and I were now twenty years closer to the age of retirement, and I was desperate to find her while we were still in our thirties.

There was no time to lose.

Of all the amusement arcades in Fleetpool, the one in which Leanne and I had amused ourselves the most was Jumbo Amusements, so I was amused to go back there and discover that this mini-casino adjacent to the dolphinarium was now called Dolphin Amusements.

The philosopher in me, naturally, began to speculate. An elephant to a fish? Is that what they call progress? Is progress inevitable? Is progress desirable? What *is* progress? Is your progress my progress? Is the subjective inherent in everything? Can anything be entirely objective? When do semiotics and semantics overlap?

Leanne and I used to purloin change from the slot machines and use the money to gain admission to the dolphinarium. There we would see families having fun, and we would mock them, as if watching dolphins performing tricks were somehow all very well for the plebians of this world but somehow beneath us. We used to guess the names of the fathers and mothers and children. "He's a Norman." "She's a Maureen." "He's a Charlie." "He's a *right* Charlie." "She's a Pauline." "He's a Darren." "No, he's more of a Gary." "She's a Sharon." "No, she's more of a Tracy." We once asked a boy of about twelve (whom we had guessed to be a Danny) what his name was. He peered at us through his thick-rimmed glasses, grimaced in contempt, and told us to "get lost".

I said earlier that we often explore the past in order better to understand ourselves and others. It was fitting, then, that the final totem of my past with Leanne that I toured was

Beach House Park and therein, particularly, the beech tree (the pun is entirely coincidental) on the trunk of which we had seen carved: "God was here. But then He's everywhere." I had crafted my name under the slogan and Leanne had chiselled hers under mine. Lo and behold, this tripartite engraving was not only still there, on public display, it had suffered little erosion at the cruel hands of the elements. Here was a case where the bark was very much better than (the elements') bite.

"The darkest hour is just before dawn."

How often do we hear Thomas Fuller's phrase declaimed to offer solace and consolation to the afflicted? My affliction was great enough on that Thursday afternoon, as I stood staring (almost weeping) at the sturdy trunk of a lone beech tree, to induce despair. I must have cut a forlorn figure as I stood there wondering why I had embarked upon such a futile mission, unable to set aside the notion that I should not return to Sudbury, to my wife, forthwith, to be home in time for our pub's happy hour, the very time at which our most regular customers were at their most entertainingly lugubrious.

Yet there was I, standing on the cusp of dawn without knowing it, my darkest hour passing away before my very eyes. Something was afoot, and it would manifest itself that Thursday evening, in the Queen's Arms. There would my breakthrough moment arrive. The spark that I needed to ignite my search for Leanne would be lit.

In the meantime, there was a police matter to deal with. It was not exactly a serious matter, but simply a matter of stumbling across a drug-dealer and his dog. On the first evening of my stay in Fleetpool, the beginning of my quest to find Leanne, in the Queen's Arms, I had got talking with a young detective, and he told me that his first major task in the job was to apprehend a one-legged man, a suspected small-time dealer of cannabis in the town, and his three-legged dog, his unsuspecting partner-in-crime. His superior officer was expecting a quick result on the presumption that uncovering such a conspicuous duo would not require the detective prowess of a Sherlock Holmes.

Three days later, I had found them for him. I was no master of surveillance. I had simply come across them as they hopped through the park when I was staring at a tree.

I took out my phone and rang the young detective on the number he had given me.

Even at that darkest hour of my search for Leanne, I had not given up hope. I was pleased that I had found someone, albeit entirely by accident, and for someone else, and I still hoped that I would find Leanne in the same way.

The man and his dog had been easy to pick out for the simple reason that they stood out.

How easy to pick out would Leanne be? Would I really be able to select her from a crowd, twenty years on? Would she be able to point me out in the same crowd?

I was asking myself these questions even after my longed-for breakthrough was past.

TEN

First Encounters

When I came to think about my first encounter with Leanne, not atypically for me, I veered off on a philosophical tangent. I am one of those people who cannot resist wondering whether the falling tree makes a sound as it falls if there is nobody present to witness the fall, or whether my bed exists when there is nobody present to see it, or whether the cow is there, in the field, when nobody is around to perceive it.

My mind immediately turned to the idea of archetypes. Is there not an archetypal me, Frankie McDowell, an indelible imprint of the essential me on the cosmic consciousness? Is there not an archetypal Leanne Kenyon? Is there not an archetypal Gwendoline Baxter? There is, without doubt, a Gwendoline Baxter *type*. So, why not a Gwendoline Baxter *archetype*? Is the Gwendoline Baxter I know not simply a facsimile of the prototype, a physical emanation of the essence, a particular Gwendoline Baxter at one remove from the Form of Gwendoline Baxter?

Archetypes, essences, and Forms: are they not, basically, one and the same thing, or so close in nature to each other as to be all but identical in their meaning and in their application?

We are talking here about the difference between *ideas* and *things.*

We experience this dichotomy on the most mundane levels, when we visit a place, for example, and find that it is a far cry from what we expected, for better or for worse.

Expectation and reality rarely match, and the difference is one of degree rather than kind.

Pondering such highbrow matters got me thinking about boundaries.

Where does a person or a place or a thing begin and end?

Let us take Leanne. What are the boundaries of the physical Leanne? Where are the limits of the spiritual Leanne? What of her soul? Presuming that she has a soul, can it be delineated? Can it be delimited? Can it, indeed, be contained? *Must* it be contained?

Is there not a place, somewhere, that is both Fleetpool and not Fleetpool?

When does the spoon become something other than the spoon?

Where is the boundary between things so nebulous as sin and virtue?

Does the boundary itself not have boundaries?

Then there is the problem of the "I": either the material "I", or the spiritual "I", or both conjoined.

Who, then, am I to use the term "I", when referring to myself, when your "you", when referring to me, is less subjective than my "I" when referring to myself?

The subjectivity here undermines the very idea of the boundary.

We can say more about boundaries by considering historical events.

Take the Japanese attack on Pearl Harbour. There was a time when the attack had not happened, and there was a time when it was a recorded, documented fact, and, at some point between these two situations, the attack began.

How, though, to determine that point, that moment, and where to place it?

History records the attack as having taken place on December 7th, 1941, but, once more, when did the attack begin? When the first bomb was dropped on the sleeping harbour on that infamous day? Sometime before? When Admiral Isoroku Yamamoto first began planning the attack? Sometime before that even? When the idea of the attack was conceived? Before that even?

We talk about people, places, things, and historical events—and even the very ideas themselves—as if they are cold, hard facts, almost as Mr Gradgrind did, because both imagination and intellect must be suspended for the sake of clarity of meaning.

Thus, even when we speak of a historical fact as cold and as hard as the Japanese attack on Pearl Harbour, we desist from invoking the realm of ideas, we refrain from tracing events back through cause and effect until we reach the first cause, the *idea*, the *very* idea, to determine *which* idea, and *whose* idea.

When Leanne and I first met, I was able to *feel* (hence my ability to paint well) but much less able to *think*.

Our first encounter came less than an hour after my arrival in Fleetpool, on the August Bank Holiday Monday of 2001. The beach was full of people taking advantage of the surprisingly warm weather; there were clouds above, but high above, and they were whisps and streaks of white, unthreatening, and the sun now and then disappeared behind them; sometimes, the obscurity was only partial, leaving the beach and the people on it enveloped by a half-shade that moved back and forth in regular swathes.

God only knows why, of all the people populating the stony beach on that day, and at that time of the afternoon, I singled out the dark-haired girl sitting with her legs pulled towards her chest, and her chin resting on her knees, gazing listlessly at the distant horizon. She was wearing black leggings and a purple fleece jacket, and she sported expensive-looking sunglasses as if optimism had got the better of her and she was expecting a surfeit of sunshine.

She looked over her left shoulder at me as if she had sensed my presence, and, for a moment, I felt like an intruder, as if I had come between her and the sea and whatever she was contemplating beyond it.

Her immediate acceptance of me was unnerving, for she simply moved the duffel bag beside her, from her left to her right side, as if to make room for me. It was as though I were a close friend—her husband or boyfriend even—and had just returned to our spot on the beach with ice-creams.

For about a minute, after I had taken my place beside her, I looked out to sea and tried to see whatever she was seeing. I saw only people thinning out in number the further away from the water's edge I looked, the sun's reflection glinting in the water at high tide, a few windsurfers, a boat or two, way out, and the horizon beyond which, I supposed, was the object of the girl's contemplation.

"Do you believe in premonitions?"

The question startled me.

"I had a feeling you were going to ask me that."

The answer impressed her.

"You were born on the fifteenth of August, nineteen-eighty-two," she declared with such disarming conviction that I knew that she had not just asked a question but made a statement.

"How do you know that?"

"I sensed it."

"You *sensed* it?"

"Yes, I'm psychic, but you won't find me on the pier gazing into a crystal ball."

"Why not? It might make you rich."

"It's not that kind of psychic."

"My name's Frankie, but I guess you knew that."

Leanne perused me awhile, examining my features and working me over in her mind; she was wondering whether I was worth so much as another second of her time.

Eventually, she told me her name.

We established that Leanne was from Oxford and that she had left her home city under something of a cloud and arrived in Fleetpool without quite knowing how.

I told her that I had enough money for somewhere to stay, indefinitely, and some work prospects, but that, presently, I was of no fixed abode.

She told me that she had been sleeping in a bandstand for the past few days, that it afforded a decent level of shelter, and that she had been sneaking into the local swimming baths to undertake her ablutions.

She then hit me with another question that came at me like a bolt out of the blue.

"Do you believe in fate?"

"Yes, there's one going on right now, on the beach green over there," I quipped. "I passed it on my way here."

"You're a comedian, aren't you?"

"Yes, but you won't find me on the seaside circuit doing standup."

We then established that I was from Sudbury, the Sudbury in Suffolk, not the Sudbury in Middlesex, or the Sudbury in Derbyshire, and that I had come to Fleetpool to suffer for my art.

Leanne suggested that Fleetpool had a strong enough vibe for the sensitive artist.

She then told me that she had been in Fleetpool for a few days, having been abandoned by a man she had met in Oxford who had promised her a new life in Kendal, in Cumbria.

"We were on our way up there. We stopped at a pub just outside Fleetpool for a bite to eat. I went to the toilet. When I came out, he was gone."

"Unbelievable!"

"You'd better believe it."

"Will you go after him?"

"Why would I do that?"

"To have it out with him?"

"I've already forgotten him. I'm here. I'm alone. That's all there is to it."

"But you're *not* alone, are you?"

She looked me over again like someone examining goods she feared might be stolen.

"Spend the night with me in the bandstand," she said, "and we'll take it from there."

Certain that I would not receive a more enticing offer that day, I accepted the invitation without hesitation.

As we have seen, Leanne and I spent but one night together in the bandstand before we were discovered by the benignant eyes of Mrs Baxter.

Naturally, on the first evening of my return, I went back to that very spot where Leanne and I had first met, the spot that chimed the loudest, not to say the most melodious, with all my cherished memories of my year with Leanne.

It was also the spot where Leanne would indulge her craze for skinny-dipping, a craze to which I had been obliged to conform.

She would throw herself into the water, naked as the day she was born, at intervals too regular for my liking, during the small hours of the morning, in the shadow of the moon-lit pier, with her trusty companion following tentatively in her wake.

The first time we took a dip in the water was one chilly night in September when it was warmer (as we discovered) in the water than it was outside. I had pleaded with Leanne, for the sake of her health as much as her modesty, not to be so daring.

I had even suggested the possibility of our being seen.

"Look around," she had said. "How many people do you see?"

I had seen none.

Even at that early stage in our friendship, I had been able to discern that, for Leanne, the pier was both reference point and sanctuary, an idea supported later by the fact that, in the year that we spent together, we never strayed more than half-a-mile from the giant structure that squatted in the sea like a beneficent behemoth.

The town itself, or that part of it to which we confined ourselves, was, to Leanne, like a womb.

By some process of psychological and emotional osmosis, her world became my world.

She assimilated me to herself and I gratefully acceded.

Essentially, then, we were one.

ELEVEN

The Queen's Arms

I found the Queen's Arms much the same as it had been two decades ago, though I suspected that the place had been refurbished at least once in the meantime. The customers had not changed, even if they were different people. The pub was lively for a Monday evening. There was a murmur of chatter as I approached the bar, and a group of young men to my right suddenly burst into song. The barmaid was another woman in her forties, and she did not look unlike Angela Palmer. I was bound to ask the question.

"She was my auntie," came the reply.

"Please don't tell me that she's passed away."

"She died a couple of years ago, doing what she did best, pulling pints."

"She died *here*?"

"Right here, where I'm standing…"

"Oh, well, I'm stunned."

It was probably for the best that the lady did not give me the chance to dwell on the shocking news, since she asked me where I was from; when I told her, she informed me that she had never been further south than Harrogate, to which I replied that she was not missing much in sticking firmly to her northern redoubt.

"What are you having, my love?"

"A pint of bitter, please…"

"What are you doing back up this way then?" The lady asked the question whilst pulling the pint with her strong-looking right arm, a feature of hers that contributed to an overall appearance of firmness of purpose and strength of mind.

"I'm looking for someone," I replied.

"That sounds rather cryptic."

"I'm certainly looking at a puzzle."

"You look like you're sickening for someone. A girl, I suppose. I hope you find her."

"She was a girl when I saw her last. She'll be a woman now."

"When I saw you walking in here, dressed in black, I thought you were one of those Mormon fellas."

"Mormon?"

"Yes, they come in here from time to time. They don't preach, but they chat with the customers—which is preaching in a way, I suppose—and scare some of them away. I have to send them packing. They're bad for business."

"I, too, run a pub, and I have the same problem with Jehovah's Witnesses."

I handed her my business card.

The lady placed my drink on the bar and told me that it was on the house, "from one publican to another". She then told me her name: Janet Shawcross.

Trying not to sound obsequious, I said that I was pleased to meet her.

The din from the lads in the corner was deafening now.

"What's all the noise about?" I enquired.

"They're fans of Fleetpool Town," Janet answered. "It was their first game of the season on Saturday. They won. They're still celebrating, since Fleetpool win so rarely. When they lose, they come in here and stare into their beer. Either way, they're good for business, unlike the Mormons."

Janet went off to serve another customer, whereupon a man of about twenty-five sidled up to me looking as though he had just won the lottery before realising that he had lost his ticket. He was standing far enough away for me to be able to ignore him without seeming rude, but close enough for me to feel guilty about ignoring him, especially as he looked so glum.

"Rough day?" I ventured to ask.

"Like you wouldn't believe," the man replied, seemingly surprised that I was giving him the time of day.

"I've had plenty of rough days."

"Connor Ableman's the name."

"Frankie McDowell…"

We shook hands.

"Detective Constable Connor Ableman," he added, "though I'm starting to ask myself if becoming a policeman was the best career move I could have made."

"It's true what they say: you know you're getting old when police officers start to look young." I was just thinking that I was some fifteen years older than him but had been some five years younger than he was now when I was on the streets in Fleetpool. "Where are you from?" He had a West Country accent.

"Penzance, Cornwall…"

"I've been there. It's a fantastic place."

"And I was posted to this fleapit!"

"The place will grow on you."

"Today's my first day in the job. I spent the morning investigating a shoplifting at a supermarket. I had to stare at CCTV footage for three long hours. I was cross-eyed by lunchtime. This afternoon, I was tasked with finding a one-legged man and his three-legged dog."

"Are they the shoplifters?"

"The one-legged man is a small-time drug-dealer in the town. He's been passing some dope and Charlie around."

"I'll keep my eyes peeled for you," I said. "If I see them, I'll let you know."

"How hard can it be to find a one-legged man wandering around with a three-legged dog?" my companion wondered aloud. "Knowing my luck, this town will be full of them."

He handed me his card as I was handing him mine.

"Where are you from, then, Frankie?"

"Sudbury, Suffolk…"

"Lovely part of the world…"

"Take out Haverhill and Suffolk would be almost perfect."

"Take Bodmin out of Cornwall and Cornwall would be paradise."

"Every county has its blot on the landscape."

"And Fleetpool must be Lancashire's blot on the landscape."

"Trust me, the place has a hidden charm that slowly reveals itself."

Connor looked over his left shoulder as if, somehow, in spite of the din of chatter and singing, not to mention his not having eyes in the back of his head, he had just been startled by someone or something entering the pub.

"Look out!" he exclaimed. "Here comes my boss!"

"Ableman!" the newcomer intoned, surprised to see his well-bred junior officer in the pub at all, never mind propping up the saloon bar. "So, this is where you spend your evenings!"

"You, too, apparently, sir!"

We three were having to raise our voices to be heard.

It was decided that it was the constable's round, and, as Connor did the honours, the senior detective turned his attention to me. His suit was immaculate, his white shirt was gleaming, and his black shoes were shining. Only the red-and-black striped tie let him down, for it was shabby and threadbare, as if he were wearing the old bashed-up thing purely for its sentimental value. I had often wondered why detectives dressed so smartly to do such a grubby job of work. He introduced himself to me as Detective Inspector David Clarkson, a name as prosaic as any police officer's had ever been. His manner of speaking was a tad pompous, as middle-ranking police officers often sound when they are trying to invest themselves with gravitas. I introduced myself in turn, before the two police officers retired to a corner to talk shop, specifically about the "disabled fugitives", as the inspector termed the one-legged man and his three-legged dog.

Connor was not exactly revelling in the extra-curricular encounter with his boss, and he kept looking over at me, enviously, as I devoured the steak-and-ale pie recommended me by our hostess, envious, I dare say, of my solitude as much as my delicious-looking evening meal.

The following evening in the Queen's Arms would be equally fruitless, in terms of my search for Leanne, though no less interesting in terms of the company I kept.

That day, the Tuesday, had been an interesting day all round (subsequent chapters will describe how and why), and the interestingness must have spilled over and contributed to my feeling of intoxication at the prospect of finding Leanne. I had come to see the entire project as just that: the *prospect*. I was drunk with excitement, exhilarated, overcome by a surge of almost unbearable optimism.

Having spent the latter part of the afternoon dozing in a deckchair on the beach, I had returned to my room, to the armchair by the window, listened to one of my albums (*Dry*, by Polly Jean Harvey) on my Discman, showered, changed, and headed for the Queen's Arms filled with expectation.

The Queen's Arms was busier than my pub usually was early on a Tuesday evening, though the seat at the bar, where I had sat the evening before, was free. I ordered a pint of bitter from the young barman and was only a minute or so into drinking it when a man of about my age planted himself beside me and began lamenting the dysfunctionality of his family life. There were no introductions, no formalities, no pleasantries, he simply threw himself into a monologue which bordered on a diatribe. He spoke whilst nursing a pint of ale, and he stopped talking only to sip from it, from time to time, as if the beer were medicinal, something to fortify him before the dreaded return to his family home.

The essence of his speech was as follows…

"My wife doesn't understand me. I don't understand my son. Do my wife and son understand each other? Oh, yes, they are absolutely on the same wavelength. They understand each other perfectly. They are always plotting against me. I'm only the mug who goes out and earns all the money to keep house and home. Without me, they wouldn't have a roof over their scheming little heads.

"My wife treats the household credit card as if it were her own personal allowance, she likes to test its flexibility in the boutiques of Manchester, flaunting it as if she were the wife of a player of City or United.

"My son has a pet rat. He named it after me. Fancy that! What does that say about the esteem in which he holds me? He never does anything, my boy. He doesn't play football. He doesn't play computer games. He's not a normal boy. All he does is sit in his room, getting paler and thinner. He looks like Iggy Pop on hunger strike. Last night, he and I talked. Hallelujah! He said to me, 'I'm an individual.' 'So you are,' I said. 'I want a new experience,' he said. I took a sniff of him and said, 'Try washing.' That's the most meaningful conversation we've ever had. How sad is that?"

The man gave me no opportunity to respond, for he disappeared before I had a chance to register what he had said.

It was another baffling encounter in a life full of baffling encounters.

Wednesday evening in the Queen's Arms was yet more surreal than the two previous evenings there had been. I toyed with the idea that the position at the bar where I was parking myself possessed surrealist properties which attracted surreal phenomena, in the way that like attracts like, or in the nature of something that, imbued with a particular quality, will attract things harbouring the very same quality.

That evening's burlesque offering came in the form of a man about thirty-five named Lucian. Before we progressed beyond the pleasantries, then, the evening had taken a surreal enough turn, since (I was bound to wonder) what were the chances of meeting an artistic-looking man named Lucian in a bawdy public house in Fleetpool? Had the man not been so young, I might have imagined that I was conversing with Lucian Freud himself.

The best way to describe my brief encounter with Lucian is to quote verbatim what passed between us.

"I'm in the most dreadful pickle, you see. I've been living what might be called a double life. I've been seeing two women—separately, you understand—and, so far, I've managed to keep the one a secret from the other. Things are coming to a head now, though, and with a vengeance, if you know what I mean."

"You mean the secret's out?"

"Not exactly…"

"But the secret soon *will* be out?"

"Oh, yes, unavoidably so. You see, I've proposed to both women. I was hoping that at least one of them would decline, but they both accepted! God, what a state I've got myself into."

"You have a decision to make, unavoidably so."

"Yes, like whether to emigrate or not to emigrate."

"Can't you simply choose which one of the women to marry, and let the other one down gently?"

"That, sadly, is not an option."

"No?"

"Whichever one I choose to marry, both women will know that I've been two-timing them, and I will end up with neither of them."

"You have no choice but to make a decision and accept the consequences."

"It gets worse."

"Oh?"

"One of the women has a brother who's a bit of a local gangster. I'm rather attached to my testicles. I'd hate to be separated from them."

"That does rather complicate matters."

"Indeed!"

"Are the two women alike?"

"God, no! That's why I'm in this dreadful mess. The two women couldn't be more different. That's always been my problem: the inability to reconcile two opposites. Emma, you see—how can I put this delicately?—is, basically, not to put too fine a point on it—oh, sod delicacy—sexy and stupid, very sexy and even more stupid. But she's pliable, you know, perfectly pliable."

"Pliable?"

"Well, you know, dutiful, wifely…"

"Oh, I see."

"Whereas Emily—God, their names are practically identical—is as unutterably beautiful as she is deliciously intelligent. Take it from me, her wit is positively impish. However, unlike Emma, Emily couldn't boil an egg. She's totally useless in the house."

"What kind of woman do you want in a wife?"

"Both! That's the problem!"

"If only bigamy were an option."

"I used to fantasise that I was a mad scientist, and that I was in love with a girl named Jane, who was ravishingly gorgeous but thick as two short planks. So, I took another woman—I called her Hannah—who was plain but had a brain the size of a planet, and I swapped her brain with Jane's. So, Jane was now gorgeous and formidably intelligent, leaving poor Hannah plain and thick. I had produced the perfect woman in Jane."

"So, what happened next in your fantasy?"

"I fell in love with Hannah!"

He went on to lament that even in his fantasies he cannot get his love-life straight. I told him that we all have our challenges in love, and that many of the challenges stem from each man's idea that he is somehow God's gift to women, a conception that is overturned by experience time after time.

To this day, I have no idea what happened to Lucian in the days and months after our chance encounter, but I would not mind betting that he is licking wounds—counting his blessings, too, perhaps—in foreign climes, somewhere, chastened, but alive, shaken, stirred, but in one piece.

As I had a dinner date with Andrea on that Wednesday evening, I took my sustenance in the pub in liquid form only.

Who is Andrea? More about her later.

Thursday—let me say it again—was the day of my coveted breakthrough, and it came in the Queen's Arms, that veritable haven of the unusual and the unexpected.

One might ask why the breakthrough would not have come in the Queen's Arms? Is the public house not the type of place where gossip is overheard, information exchanged, and deals done? Public houses are like golf courses, only more illicit. Any police officer would vouch for the intelligence-gathering potential of the public house.

The agent of my breakthrough was a man of some forty years named Tommy. He was dressed elegantly, and he spoke calmly and not without refinement. If I were to guess his profession, I would say he was a graphic designer, for he had about him the air of both artist and technician.

Somehow, from the beginning of my scheme to find Leanne—from its conception, through its inception, to its execution—I had known that a breakthrough *would* present itself to me.

"If I ask enough people enough questions then, eventually, I'll find Leanne."

That was my avowed strategy, and I trusted that it would serve me well.

Up to a point…

Up to the point where Providence was bound to intervene.

If I were to help myself then Providence would help me.

I would be empowered to make my own luck.

Providence would expect nothing less.

That was the deal.

That is *always* the deal.

On that Thursday evening, I sat not on my usual high stool at the bar, in the vortex of surrealism, but in a dark corner, a murky shadow, into which murky shadow, from some other murky shadow, like an emerging avatar, stepped Tommy, a man brimming with anticipation at the prospect of doing something pleasurable but illicit.

He was in the right place for that.

He told me that he had overheard part of my conversation with Lucian the previous evening, that part of the conversation when I had told my erstwhile companion that I had come to Fleetpool to search for someone, and when I had asked him if he had ever heard the name Leanne Kenyon mentioned in Fleetpool.

Tommy informed me that he knew someone who knew someone who knew Leanne—or who *had* known her—and that he, Tommy, had heard, many years ago, from this extended grapevine, that Leanne had left Fleetpool to take up a job in Hebden Bridge, at the Bridgehead Hotel, which, he assured me, was still in existence.

In return for this precious information, I bought Tommy a drink.

Then I bought him another.

It was not much, but it was something, an opening, a foot in the door of a huge castle where Leanne might be hidden.

I was on Leanne's trail.

TWELVE

Leanne

She had lived with her Uncle Leo since she was ten years old, after her parents died in a car crash, and had left home, at the age of nineteen, to escape the clutches of the cold, austere man who had been her legal guardian but who had signally abdicated his responsibility as the custodian of her morals.

The man was a good deal more than cold and austere, he was downright cruel, and the cruelty was not of the physical kind either. It was worse than that: it was psychological, and it was relentless, a daily drip-feed of depraved pressure on the head and the heart that would wound, injure, and otherwise damage, permanently.

I had told Leanne—for this is the basis of *her* story—in a moment of supreme tactlessness, that there were people in the world even worse off than she was. There were folk in Africa whose eyes had been eaten out by insects. There were people all over the world with horrible deformities, disabilities, and disfigurements. To her disbelief (though it was true), I had told her about one of the boys in my class at school, whose father had had a sex-change and become his mother, and whose mother had had a sex-change and become his father, a dual transformation from which he had never recovered, so that he was languishing now in a hospital for the mentally disturbed, while his parents were busy sunning themselves in a retirement villa in the Costa del Sol.

Leanne must have asked me a thousand times if that latter story were true.

Three anecdotes concerning Leanne's Uncle Leo and his callous treatment of her are enough to demonstrate what she endured as a child, and to reveal thereby a character that is both profoundly sensitive and uncommonly resilient.

"Most of the time, my Uncle Leo was okay," Leanne had once told me, "but the rest of the time he was an evil bastard." She had added that it was the not knowing when he would switch to being evil that would compound the terror once the switch was made.

"I'm sorry," I had said feebly.

"He used to lock me in my room."

"How often?"

"Too often!"

"Why did he do that?"

"Because he was a sick pervert. He used to say that he would let me out once I'd stopped having 'impure' thoughts about him."

"Impure?"

"You know, thoughts, *sexual* thoughts …"

"He accused you of that? That's insane!"

"Talk about twisting things …"

"Did he ever, you know, *touch* you?"

"No, which, in a way, made his behaviour even sicker."

"Sick is the word."

"Of course, I had to go along with what he said, say what he wanted me to say, just to be let out of the room."

"Did he ever marry?"

"He was engaged once. His fiancée disappeared one day and was never seen again. Rumour had it that he killed her and buried her somewhere."

"Sounds plausible…"

Another time, Leanne described how her uncle used to spy on her when she was in the bathroom.

"Whenever I went into the bathroom, he would go into his bedroom, and I would hear his wardrobe being moved sideways. His bedroom was next to the bathroom. There was a little spyhole in the wall which I couldn't cover with a towel or anything. He'd made it look like a hole for a nail for hanging a picture, but I could tell what it was, and, anyway, who hangs pictures in the bathroom? Through that spyhole, he could see the whole of the bathroom. The shower was in the bath, and there was no curtain or anything. One day, when he was out, I went into his bedroom, moved his wardrobe aside, and there it was: the spyhole. For eight, nine years, he was watching me. It makes me sick just thinking about it."

One afternoon, we were wallowing in deckchairs under the July sun, when Leanne gave me an even more disturbing account of her uncle's behaviour, one that made me physically sick, and I am a person who lost his innocence at about the same time that Leanne lost hers, so shocking me should have been all but impossible.

"He took me on holiday once. Anglesey, it was. Arse-end of the universe. A million miles from anywhere. Some remote farmhouse. Out in public, he made me pretend to be his girl, his woman, his wife, whatever."

"Why did he do that?"

"He booked the holiday there because he knew some neighbours of ours had a holiday home there."

"How do you mean?"

"Robert and Christine Moorhouse, who lived a couple of houses down the street, they had a second home on Anglesey, and they always spent the first and second weeks of August there."

"You think he wanted these people to see you and him together?"

"Yep…"

"But Anglesey—it's an island, isn't it?—well, it's a pretty big place, so the chances of running into your neighbours must have been pretty small."

"One day, we ran into them in Rhosneigr. He seemed to know that they would be there. God knows how, but he did. They saw us holding hands."

"What did they say when they saw you?"

"They were really embarrassed, and they looked disgusted."

"How old were you at the time?"

"Fifteen…"

"So, word got around your neighbourhood that you and your uncle were the best of friends?"

"No, because Robert and Christine must have kept quiet about it, but they never spoke to us again, and Uncle Leo slaughtered me for making him look like a pervert."

"But *he* forced *you!*"

"I know, but that's how he operated."

"You should have left him."

"I *did* leave him!"

"I mean sooner, a *lot* sooner …"

"Well, it's done now."

It is often said, usually figuratively, to indicate an accentuated degree of adulation, that somebody worships the very ground upon which another person walks.

That is precisely how I felt about Leanne when we were together, and when I went in search of her, and that is how I will feel about her until the day I die.

More, I worship the very air that she breathes.

As I made my discombobulated way around Fleetpool on my return trip, as I toured all the places where Leanne and I had been, my pulse raced and raced as I was transported back two decades to that long hour of bliss, the one time in my life when I was truly happy.

I was truly happy because my love for Leanne was as true as truth itself.

As I sought out Leanne, every square inch of the ground bore her imprint, and the very air was infused with her spirit.

Nobody but Leanne has ever moved me to feel that way.

My memory of her and all that she touched is sacred.

What else could my love for her be but true?

THIRTEEN

Mehmed

On the Monday evening, I had sought out Sultan Kebab and found it exactly where it had been twenty years before. It was even more blighted by ugly neon lighting than it had been back then: the colours were so loud that the place was as much a cacophony of sound as a garish eyesore.

My old friend Mehmed would be the first to agree that his establishment was not exactly a paragon of the understated.

I had peered through the window, to see if Mehmed was there, but had seen only a man of about the same age as Mehmed had been two decades before.

Having resolved to return to the shop first thing next morning, I arrived at about ten-thirty on the Tuesday and walked into an altercation between a cutglass-accented middle-aged gentleman in a green Barbour jacket and a young man of Middle Eastern extraction standing on the other side of the counter. It was the most unlikely encounter I would ever witness. The banter was going to and fro.

"Mehmed will be here tomorrow. You can take it up with him then."

"I'm not waiting until tomorrow."

"Okay, so how can *I* help you?"

"You can give me my money back."

"But the satnav works."

"It *doesn't* work. Mehmed sold me a satnav a month ago, but the thing was a duffer. Whichever address I put in the machine, it directed me to Mehmed's brother's carpet shop, which wouldn't have been a problem so much had I wanted a Turkish carpet. So, I complained, whereupon Mehmed gave me a new satnav, but that, too, disregards whichever address I enter and diverts me to Mehmed's brother's carpet shop. I had to go and see a new client in Carlisle the other day. I put in the address details, but, lo and behold, I ended up outside Mehmed's brother's carpet shop."

"Mehmed must have had a faulty batch."

"Either that or the satnavs became befuddled when they fell off the back of a lorry."

"We don't run that kind of racket, my friend."

"Can't I just have my money back?"

"Look, I'll call my dad and he'll bring the money to you this evening."

"Right, okay, that'll do."

"In the meantime, as a gesture of goodwill, I can offer you anything you like from the shop, free of charge."

"I wouldn't stoop to eating anything from *this* place, though, I have to say, that avocado mousse doesn't look half bad."

"That's mushy peas."

"In that case, I'll pass. I'll expect Mehmed this evening then."

"Count on it, sir."

With that, the man was gone.

"Are you Mehmed's son?" I asked the young man once the fallout from the incongruous exchange had settled.

"That's right, boss. The name's Ali. What can I do for you?"

He looked nervous, as if I might be a creditor, or an official from Environmental Health, or a police officer.

"I was hoping to speak with Mehmed."

"Don't tell me, he sold you a dodgy satnav, and you want your money back?"

If only I had a celestial satnav that would take me to Leanne, I thought.

"Nothing like that," I said. "My name's Frankie McDowell. Mehmed and I are old friends."

"Oh, yeah, boss. My old man talks about you. You and some lass."

"Actually, she's one of the reasons why I want to talk with Mehmed. He was good to us way back."

"He's a good man, my dad, when he's not offloading hooky merchandise. That bloke who was here just now is the third person this week who's come in here wanting his money back after buying a dodgy satnav from my dad. I keep telling him to stick to selling kebabs."

"Where's your dad now?"

"We've got another place, a new place, up at Graduate Heights. He's working there today."

"That's convenient, since I was going up there, anyway."

"Do you want me to give him a bell, to let him know you're coming?"

"No, thanks, I think I'll surprise him."

"Right you are, boss."

"Thanks for your help, Ali. Have a good day."

"Mind how you go, boss."

Though Fleetpool that day had woken up to a storm, the tempest had been appeased by some privately-spoken petition, and was now reduced to a swirling drizzle carried by a stiff breeze which now and then surged to a gust blasting off the sea like a broadside from a battleship. There were a few brave souls about, determined not to let a minor hurricane interfere with their holiday plans. There were figures dotted about the beach, prodding the wet sand with forks and spades, looking (I suspected) for worms for fishing bait, and others poking at rockpools with sticks, uncovering crabs out of curiosity for the creatures and their habitat. Beyond these silhouetted figures, the vast black plains of the sea rolled in relentlessly, and without remorse, carrying with its awesome rumble a warning to get out of the way or be consumed. Such was the perfidious way that the sea at Fleetpool came in and encircled unsuspecting beachcombers and strollers that the people out on the sand at that moment would have been well-advised to heed the warning without delay.

The previous evening, as I was returning to my room after my long day, the manager of the hotel, Selwyn Wyatt-Jones, had stopped me by the reception desk and greeted me with an accent that was both Scottish brogue and Welsh lilt, a bit of Aberdeen with an infusion of Abergavenny.

"Good evening, Mr McDowell!"

The man was immaculately dressed in crisp white shirt, tie, grey slacks, and black corporate blazer. He looked like an airline pilot. I walked over to him, studied his name badge, and returned his greeting.

"Are you enjoying your stay in Fleetpool?" he asked me.

"It's good to be back," I replied.

"Nadine was telling me that you're looking for a Mrs Gwendoline Baxter."

"I am, but I doubt that I'll find her."

"I think I can help you there."

"Really?"

"She's now the proprietor of the Linton Lodge Guest House, up the hill, in Graduate Heights."

"Oh, thanks so much for the information," I gushed, trying hard not to look like a child on Christmas Day surveying a heap of unwrapped presents. "That's fantastic. I did look her up online, but there was no trace of her. There's been much too much water under the bridge since I was here last."

"She remarried and goes by a different name now."

"I'm made up for her. She deserves to be happy."

"Her first husband died, of course."

"Yes, way back, before I knew her."

"She's Gwendoline Watkins now."

"I'll go and see her tomorrow. I can't thank you enough for the information."

At the time, it had seemed like a breakthrough delivered by the invisible but ever-trusty hand of Providence; that it would prove not to be so did not occur to me; and I had gone to bed fatigued but almost too excited to sleep.

During my previous sojourn in Fleetpool, I had heard much about Graduate Heights without ever learning where the "Graduate" part of the name came from. There was no university at the top of the hill, only a secondary school, and

I doubted that that institution alone would justify an invocation of academic excellence of any kind. Graduate Heights was select, the most salubrious quarter of town, the Beverley Hills of Fleetpool. I knew that much. The streets were not paved with gold. I knew that much too. But I reckoned that they were not littered with canine faeces, either, as many of the streets in the town centre were.

Twice, on my way up the hill, I had to perform difficult hill-starts at traffic lights, and the second time I had almost rolled backwards and hit the car behind me.

I had decided to see Mehmed first, knowing that there would be little or no chance that he would be able to give me any information as to Leanne's whereabouts, so that my visit would amount to little more than a social call, albeit one that I looked forward to immensely.

I would happily have visited both Mehmed and Mrs Baxter even had I known that neither would have been able to help me in my hunt for Leanne.

These two people were as sacred to me as the ground upon which Leanne had walked, and which I worshipped.

Unaccountably, I was nervous about seeing mine and Leanne's erstwhile hostess, Mrs Baxter, but I parked those nerves with my car outside Sultan Kebab, the Graduate Heights branch.

When I strode into the shop, the mutual recognition was immediate, as though twins, separated for many years, had been brought back together.

"Oh, my God, it's young Frankie!"

"Not so young anymore," I said with a smile as wide as the Thames Estuary.

"You haven't changed a bit, my friend!"

Mehmed was talking as if he *had* just been reunited with his long-lost twin brother, with a mixture of ecstasy and wonderment, barely able to contain himself. I had expected a warm welcome, but not to be overwhelmed by some joyful force of nature. He came over to me, from the other side of the counter, and gave me the tightest of bearhugs, almost lifting me off my feet as he squeezed me; when he slapped me on the back, he almost winded me, leaving me panting and heaving amid the excitement.

"You've gone up in the world," I wheezed, "quite literally."

"Yeah, the Sultan of Fleetpool, that's me!" Mehmed gestured with an outstretched arm, like Moses with his rod, at the blonde girl standing behind the counter, who was observing proceedings circumspectly, as if my sudden arrival might somehow conspire to cause her extra work. "Trudy," he said, "this is my old friend, Frankie, whom I haven't seen for, what, twenty years?"

"It's been *that* long," I confirmed.

Trudy and I acknowledged each other formally, with fixed smiles, and I wondered if she was alive when last I had seen Mehmed. It was touch and go. She looked too intelligent to be serving junk food for a living.

"Let's go upstairs for a chat," Mehmed urged, before leading me up a staircase that was littered with mops and buckets and sundry other bits and pieces of a cleaner's inventory, and the smell, a mixture of damp mopheads and chlorine, made me cough and my eyes water.

Over several cups of strong Turkish coffee, Mehmed and I chatted about how our lives had progressed in the intervening twenty years. His life had been a natural progression of business expansion, marriage, and children; and mine a sudden leap from bohemian artiness to marital respectability, prosperity, and making do without the children that both my wife and I had wanted. Guilt was stabbing at me again. My marriage was little more than a case of a woman of the world taking in a drifting dreamer of a man and giving him some direction in life, an unlikely fusion of business acumen and fevered imagination. The sense of guilt stemmed from my feeling that I was the principal beneficiary of the arrangement, and by some distance. Whichever way I looked at my marriage, for it was possible to regard it as the "perfectly serviceable relationship" unburdened by love about which my father had often spoken, I felt guilty about the betrayal of my wife in indulging myself with my pursuit of Leanne. An additional source of guilt was that I was the reason why Donna was unable to conceive. We had not given up hope of having a child, but it was getting late, the train of parenthood about to leave the station and take itself elsewhere. Guilt was coming at me from all angles as I talked with Mehmed, imploring me to give up my futile search for a ghost and return home to my wife. At that time of my life, however, my need to find Leanne—or, failing that, to find out what had happened to her—outweighed considerably the guilt that I harboured about the effect that my amateur sleuthing must have been having on my wife. It was no exaggeration to say that I was being quietly driven by a madman who had taken possession of me and all that I had worked for and held dear. I was at the mercy of this alien usurper of my being who seemed disinclined to show the slightest forbearance.

When I invited Mehmed and his wife to Suffolk, he accepted gladly, and joked that he would feel more at home there since it was closer to his ancestral homeland than was

Fleetpool. He had often invoked the unfathomable mystery that was the providence of Allah, the almighty and merciful, when explaining to me how his family, hailing from the banks of the Bosphorus, had come to be in a rundown seaside town in the north of England and practically in the Arctic Circle. He insisted that he would rather be nowhere else but Fleetpool, a town to which he owed everything, and to which he would repay everything.

If it were possible for Mehmed to have been an even better man than the man who had taken care of me and Leanne twenty years ago, with his regular donations of food and utterances of wise counsel, he *was* that man.

That he sold faulty satnavs, and was loath to refund aggrieved customers, made but a small dent in the esteem in which I held him.

He was very much of the "loveable rogue" type.

Eventually, Mehmed pointed at the elephant in the room. The creature had not been doing much to draw attention to itself. It had not been stamping its feet. It had not been trumpeting its presence. But it had been standing there, voluminously, much too big to be ignored.

"Listen, man, I'm sorry about what happened to Leanne … and to you."

"Never mind me," I replied. "What did you hear about Leanne?"

"There was something in the local rag about what happened at Splash Point. It was all rather vague. The report named both of you, and described what happened, saying that you rescued Leanne after, apparently, she had tried to commit suicide. It said that you were both of no fixed abode, and that you were both in good hands following your ordeal."

"What happened to Leanne afterwards?"

"I knew that you and Leanne used to stay at Marine Gardens Guest House, and that you used to talk about the proprietor there, Mrs Baxter, so I called her, and she had no idea where either of you was. She said she'd called all the local hospitals, but they wouldn't tell her anything, saying that, because she wasn't the legal guardian of either of you, they could give no information as to your whereabouts. She was distressed. She was very fond of you both."

"At the risk of sounding trite, we were the children she never had."

"And what was she to you?"

"An auntie figure, a kind of archetypal matriarch, I suppose…"

"You talk differently now, man, you use bigger words."

"I did an Open University degree in Philosophy, that's why."

"I bet you got a distinction."

"I did, as it happens."

"Why philosophy?"

"Well, one, I wanted to get a degree, and, two, I wanted to understand life. I thought that if I got the theory right then I might get the practice right too."

"You've done well for yourself, Frankie. I'm so proud of you, man."

"I have to give Donna much of the credit."

"She sounds like a good woman, your Donna."

"She's the best."

"I look forward to meeting her."

"And I look forward to meeting *your* wife."

"Look, Trudy needs to have her break, so I'd better go back downstairs, but, tell me, why did you leave Fleetpool without saying goodbye?"

I sighed as I recalled those heady days of intermittent consciousness, emotional turmoil, and general disorientation. They were the days of a different age; of a different person too. Sometimes, I struggle to reconcile the two people. On that August Bank Holiday Monday, twenty years ago, a new person was born. My life reached a watershed when Providence delivered me and carried me in a new direction, towards a better place, though a place without my beloved Leanne. At times, it was easy to curse Providence and wonder if it had my best interests at heart.

"When I came to at the hospital, I'd been unconscious, on and off, for twenty-four hours. The doctors asked me if there was someone who could come and collect me: preferably, my next of kin. I gave them my brother Irving's number and the next day I was back in Suffolk, determined to reshape my life. Leanne, Mrs Baxter, yourself, everyone and everything here in Fleetpool: it was as though it had all been a dream. So, that's how I chose to see it all. I left it all behind. Because I had to. To start again, I had to forget it all, even Leane; except that, as you can see, I haven't been able to forget her."

"Is she the reason you're back here?"

"The *main* reason, yes. The *only* reason, if I'm honest."

"Do you know where she is?"

"I was hoping that *you* would have some idea where she is."

"Sorry, man, I've no idea, though I can ask around for you."

"I appreciate that, thanks, but I won't get my hopes up. She's gone. That's what my head tells me. My heart tells me otherwise."

"Where do you go from here?"

"I'm going to see Mrs Baxter, or Mrs Watkins as she is now. She remarried. She's now the proprietor of the Linton Lodge Guest House, up here in Graduate Heights."

"That's fantastic for her! I'll have to go and see her. I'd like to meet her. Twenty years too late, but better late than never."

"She's my best chance of finding Leanne, but even that's a slim hope."

"Does she know you're coming?"

"I'll give her a bell now."

"You do that, my friend. See you downstairs."

FOURTEEN

Gwendoline Baxter

As I waited for Mrs Baxter (I could not call her by any other name) to answer the door of the Linton Lodge Guest House, I was hoping that the energy she had expended in response to my phone call of half-an-hour before would have left her spent, with nothing else to give in the expression of her surprise, her shock, her disbelief, that it could possibly have been me calling, as though I were a Lazarus-like figure risen from the dead; in the event, upon seeing me, she had been yet more effusive in her outpouring of incredulity and shocked exuberance than she had been when she heard my voice on the phone.

For one long disconcerting moment she had stood in the doorway, her hands clasped together in supplication, her torso wrapped tightly in an apron, intoning, mantra-like: "*Is* it you? *Can* it be you? Tell me I'm not dreaming!"

"You're not dreaming," was my rather supine response.

She had aged but only to the extent that she looked a slightly jaded version of her former self, as if the colour photograph of her had faded a little, whilst leaving the image essentially untouched. Her voice was the same, as were her mannerisms, the most noteworthy of which were her high-pitched exultations, which always came at me like the wailings of a benevolent banshee.

Once we had got as far as her living-room, she gazed at me awhile in astonishment, put a hand to my face, repeated her doorstep manta, and then burst into tears.

For some time, as my hostess wept, I felt as if *I* were the host and had just admitted a distressed loved-one into my home. I comforted her by placing a hand on her shoulder. The idea came to mind that the only discomfort she was feeling was the sense that she might be hallucinating or even suddenly prone to delusions.

My sudden appearance, it seemed, was too much for her to take in.

"You sit yourself down, my lovely, and I'll make us a nice cup of tea."

He words were soothingly familiar; they took me back twenty years and reminded me that she had shown me and Leanne such tremendous kindness that we could never hope to repay her.

We had been so much like children to her that she had even taken to tucking us into our beds at night. She used to call us "my lovelies" and "my beauties".

I was taken back to our first encounter with Mrs Baxter …

"What have we here then?" the lady had wondered aloud in an accent that was both Scouse and Mancunian, and somehow a synthesis of the proletarian and the bourgeois. "You two are coming home with me," she added, commandingly, as if she were a senior officer giving an order to subordinates.

The part of her that was not redoubtable auntie was hospital matron, and her manner, though austere, was just about benign enough to endow her with a moral authority that could not be questioned, never mind contradicted.

So, home with her we had gone, leaving the homely bandstand behind, and we were duly allocated room six to use whenever we wanted it and for as long as we needed it. Mrs Baxter never told us why that room was never reserved for guests. We assumed that it was somehow unfit for commercial use, infested with cockroaches, perhaps, or blighted by damp or mould, but we found the place spotless and insect-free, the sole deficiency a dripping tap in the basin in the bathroom. Leanne, initially, had been reluctant to accede to Mrs Baxter's charity, seeing it as an affront to the independence that she had taken to the road to assert. I had offered to pay the going rate for the room—I was able easily to afford it—but our hostess would not hear of it.

Thus had begun the pattern of our lives: living at the guest house, interspersed with periods on the streets occasioned by Leanne's periodic disappearing acts, which often left us under the stars for weeks at a time, until I was able to persuade her to return to the guest house, or Leanne became exhausted, whichever occurred sooner.

Mrs Baxter had once asked me why I did not find myself a job. I had replied that, if I were to become enmeshed in a salaried routine, I would lose Leanne, for she was not ready for domesticity, and certainly not in Fleetpool. My precarious life in Fleetpool had become bound up with her. Had I even hinted at settling down, she would simply have drifted away.

As I sat there, in the living-room of the Linton Lodge Guest House, reflecting on the past, it should have been *me* crying.

Mrs Baxter was in her kitchen.

I had drunk too much coffee with Mehmed. I was about to drink too much tea with Mrs Baxter.

We caught up with each other and our lives within twenty minutes (which represented one minute for every year since we had last seen each other) by reeling off the edited highlights, the salient details, the life-changing events, and we could not have been more pleased for each other. For Mrs Baxter, my story was heartwarming and uplifting, though she struggled to get her head around the painter-turned-publican twist in my life. To me, Mrs Baxter's account signalled affirmation that the best people could be rewarded with the best fortune, and nobody deserved good fortune more than she. When her first husband, Ronnie, had passed away, she had been left bereft. Though stoical by disposition, she had had to nurse a heart all but broken by grief. "Nobody," she had once told me and Leanne, "could ever replace my darling Ronnie." "But Johnny," she was telling me now, "well, he was such a gentleman that I could not say no to him when he asked me if I would do him the great honour of becoming his wife."

I told Mrs Baxter that, when I heard that her new name was Watkins, I had not associated her with Johnny Watkins, but that now, thinking of the two of them together, married, made perfect sense.

Mrs Baxter then joked that Johnny Watkins' wishing to be married to *any* woman was a most unlikely proposition, given that he was wedded to his beloved boatyard, and always would be.

"How did you two meet?" I asked.

"It was five years ago. His boatyard was flooded after a storm, and his flat at the yard was damaged, so he came to stay here as a paying guest—though I stopped charging him after a week—while his flat was being restored. We became friends and, before we knew what had happened, we were married."

"Just like that!"

"Well, you don't mess about at our age."

"You and Johnny are a perfect fit."

"We've talked about you and Leanne. He said that you two used to do odd jobs around the yard. I never knew that."

"Yes, Johnny used to pay us for our work. We enjoyed painting the boats. He used to tell us stories about his sailing trips, and, well, give us the benefit of his wisdom. He gave us some inspirational pep talks, just like you used to do."

"You'll go and see him, won't you?"

I said I would, and I did, the following day, Wednesday, at lunchtime. Over lunch, at the boatyard, Johnny told me that he was pleased to see that I had grown into a man of the world, since, when I was younger, he had been unable to tell whether I was male or female. "You and Leanne looked like a couple of lasses," he said. "Even now, you look rather androgynous, a cross between Marc Bolan and David Bowie," he added with his trademark throaty laugh, as if he had swallowed a cheese-grater and was trying to breathe.

Johnny had the knack of putting people at their ease with his gentle but authoritative manner; and he talked only about what he knew, never speculating or indulging in verbal perambulations. He was the very embodiment of Wittgenstein's dictum: "Whereof one cannot speak, thereof one must be silent."

Though his philosophy was rooted in experience, if I were to place him under the aegis of any one school of thought, it would not be empiricism so much as stoicism. Johnny Watkins was Kipling's poem *If* made flesh, a man who would have kept his head even had he been an aristocrat during the worst excesses of the French Revolution.

To each his or her domain. In the same way that Mehmed looked so at home in his kebab shop that one could not envisage him anywhere else, so it was for Mrs Baxter in her guest house. She was born for domesticity, but a domesticity that was more public than private, a shared domesticity, one that was welcoming and rooted in humble service. The people who came to her guest house were, indeed, *guests*, staying in her *house*. They were not customers.

When I think of Mrs Baxter, I envision the supreme competence of one doing what she was born to do, allied with the fellowship of one knowing that her qualities were given her for the personal enrichment of whomsoever she touched. It is inconceivable that she was not conscious of her endowment, though also impossible to imagine that she dwelt on its nature for long enough to become puffed up by it. She was entirely free of pride.

She gave of herself much. She demanded—she expected—nothing in return.

Suitably, given that they were married, Johnny Watkins and Mrs Baxter were two of a kind, for he, too, exuded the competence of one born for a particular vocation, effortlessly assuming his place in society, without so much as a thought as to what else he might be doing.

He was where he was, doing what he was doing, and that is all there was to it.

In his boatyard, building boats and fixing boats, amid the apparent jumble of part-built and part-fixed boats, that is where he belonged, and within that arena everything he touched bent to his will.

To each his or her domain, indeed.

Put Mehmed in the boatyard, Mrs Baxter in the kebab shop, and Johnny Watkins in the guest house, and the earth would stop spinning on its axis and the stars would fall out of the sky.

The conversation turned to the immediate aftermath of mine and Leanne's hospitalisations, after I had plucked Leanne out of the sea, and we covered the same ground over which Mehmed and I had trodden earlier.

I was left hoping against hope that Mrs Baxter might yet have some idea where Leanne was now.

"I'm sorry that we lost touch," I said.

"Oh, I understand. Like you said, you needed to start afresh. You did what you needed to do."

"Am I doing the right thing now, in coming back here to look for Leanne?"

"If it's what you need to do then yes …"

"I need to find her."

"Have you *any* idea where she is?"

I shook my head.

Mrs Baxter sighed her sadness, a sadness with its root in the events of twenty years ago, but with branches that, though withered, stretched all the way to the present.

"I was so distraught about what happened to you two that I lost my mind for a while, and I lost track of time," she said.

"Like I said, I tried to find out where you both were, but I ran into a wall, so I wallowed, and I kept wallowing, and, by the time I regained my bearings, you were gone."

"Leanne didn't contact you?"

"No, and for the same reasons you didn't, I shouldn't wonder. But I understand. It's often the way, Frankie: people meet, they meet for a reason, they have their time together, the reason for their meeting passes, and they drift apart."

"That's true," I said. "All the same, I'm sorry that Leanne and I, individually and as a couple, lost touch with you."

"*Were* you a couple?"

"We had *something*. It's hard to say what it was."

"And you want it back?"

"No, I…I simply want to know that she's okay."

"Is that what you're telling people?"

"That's what I'm telling *myself*."

"Do you think you'll find her?"

I shook my head again. I looked up and saw tears in Mrs Baxter's eyes. It seemed that she was as desperate for me to find Leanne as I was. I was moved by her desperation.

"While there's hope, I won't give up," I said. "I've given myself until next Monday to find her, our fortieth birthdays."

"Wouldn't it be wonderful if you found her on that *very* day?"

"This isn't Hollywood," I said with a laugh.

"What's your plan?"

"I've been here since yesterday afternoon. I've seen a few people, asked a few questions, and I've a few more people to see and a few more questions to ask. It all seems so hopeless, so why do I have an almost palpable sense that Leanne's here, somewhere nearby, and that I'm destined to find her?"

"I believe in you."

"That means the world to me."

"*Leanne* means the world to *you*."

"Yes," I replied, my voice trembling with emotion.

"Go and find her!"

"I will."

"When you find her, please would you remember me to her?"

"Of course, I will …"

At that, Mrs Baxter shed more tears, and I took my leave of her eager to avert another flooding, this time on *her* premises.

FIFTEEN

Splash Point

My reacquaintance with the infamous Splash Point came on the Wednesday morning after a restless night.

I was not sleeping at all well.

Like most people, I rarely sleep well in a strange bed. I would blame that on the unfamiliar surroundings and the effect they often have on one's inner compass. Another suspect is the bed and its reluctance to grant a good night's rest to someone likely to be little more than a passing acquaintance.

Only the hypnotic sound of the rhythmic caress of the sea beyond the hotel window was affording me any kind of satisfying rest.

I took breakfast in the hotel restaurant. A few fellow diners kept me company. Among them was an elegantly dressed lady of about sixty who resembled a down-at-heel duchess forced to slum it with the peasants. Our eyes met across the capacious room several times, and at one point I was convinced that she was about to join me at my table.

Her attention was unnerving.

I had no idea how I would feel about being back at Splash Point until I got there. I felt surprisingly little, except during the breathless moment when I relived what had happened there during the small hours of the August Bank Holiday Monday, twenty years ago. I had not been a hero; and, though I had done it for Leanne, I would have done it for anyone. Anyone would have. I recalled the first sensation as I hit the water and swam out to the flailing Leanne. It had been one of surprise at how easy it was to swim at a part of the beach where swimming was forbidden. Where were the strong currents and the riptide and the notorious whirlpool that would suck one down into the underworld? At high tide, I had swum over to the stricken Leanne, grabbed her, and dragged her back to the shore, where she and I, exhausted, had passed out.

Adrenaline had eased my passage to her.

How Leanne and I had from that juncture been separated with such finality was a mystery that had been only partly explained to me. That was another reason why I was in Fleetpool: to solve the mystery and so give myself closure.

The wind had got up again and was whipping up the sea behind me.

The tide was coming in now and the sea was made angry by the strong wind that was blowing rain and salty sea-spray across the promenade and into the doors of Splash Point Café, making them rattle and shudder with such startling vigour that I feared they would be blown off their hinges.

The only person in the café was the stocky man standing behind the counter looking for something to do.

"Good morning, squire!" he exclaimed, visibly excited to see a customer.

I tried to remember when someone had last called me "squire".

"Another scorcher!" he added with a chuckle.

"What's the weather been like up here this summer?" I asked.

"It's been pretty good," the man replied, "so I can't complain about this filthy weather, and the forecast is good for the Bank Holiday weekend."

"It's like winter out there at the moment."

Though I was wearing a black waterproof jacket with a hood, I was still substantially underdressed for the conditions outside; inside, the café was so warm and snug that I wondered if the heating might not be on.

"The only customers I get in here today will be blown in."

"If it's any consolation to you, I *chose* to come in."

I sat down at the table right in the centre of the café and immediately felt exposed by all the space around me. I felt like someone who had turned up an hour early for a party.

I ordered a cappuccino.

The man was slightly too big for the T-shirt he was wearing, but that served only to emphasise the muscularity of his physique. His arms were thicker than my legs. He seemed incongruous performing so delicate a task as making a cup of frothy coffee, and the mug in his spade-like hands looked much like a thimble would have looked in my delicate artist's paws.

"Where you in the army?" I asked.

"Is it that obvious?"

"You *do* have a military bearing."

"Once a soldier, always a soldier. You never quite shake it off."

"Which regiment?"

"Parachute…"

"You must have some stories to tell."

"I did two tours of duty in Northern Ireland. I left the army after the Good Friday Agreement. Not much happened when I was out there, but there was always the *threat* of violence. When a British soldier went out on patrol, he had a target on his back. We were pretty much sitting ducks. It was like walking through a minefield not knowing what you might step on."

I was talking with a man who had known *real* fear. I was humbled.

"Still, two tours of duty in Ulster must make Saturday nights in Fleetpool look rather tame in comparison?" I suggested.

"You'd be surprised, my friend. I have to think twice before venturing into town on a Saturday night. All the riff-raff pours in from the housing estates, gets pissed up, and turns the place into a warzone."

"Isn't that the case all over the country on Saturday nights?"

"This town is feral, I'll tell you that for nothing."

"Are you from Fleetpool?"

"No, I'm from Southport. That's a different kettle of fish entirely, much more genteel, but I couldn't afford to buy a place there."

"How long have you been here?"

"Fifteen years, give or take…"

"I used to come to this café, twenty-odd years ago, when I lived here."

"You from down south?"

"Suffolk…"

"Lovely!"

"It has its charms."

"What brings you back here?"

"A girl…"

"I should have guessed."

The man placed an authentic-looking cappuccino on the table. In manufacturing the substance with his machine armed with taps and valves and tubes, he had made the usual voluble hissing and squirting noises; it never ceased to amaze me that, to make something so insubstantial as a milky coffee, a café needed an apparatus resembling an oil refinery, and one that in motion sounded like a steam train in a hurry.

"What's it like owning a café right next to the most notorious spot on the beach?"

"To be honest, it's good for business."

"You'd think that such a dangerous spot would be cordoned off in some way, put out of bounds," I said.

"There's a big sign out there telling bathers to keep out."

"I know, but that seems only to encourage people to try their luck."

"There's always one. Like whenever there's a storm, there's always one idiot standing at the far end of the pier, admiring the view, who's then left wondering why he ends up in the drink."

"Have there been any incidents at Splash Point recently?"

"Three deaths so far this year. One of them left a suicide note. The other two might as well have."

"There are suicides and there are people with a death-wish."

"What's your name, squire?"

"Frankie McDowell…"

"My name's Paddy Ireland," the man declared, "and, believe it or not, I'm not Irish."

"I know a Mike England who's Welsh, a Matt Holland who's Irish, and a Jason Scotland who's Jamaican."

"What's in a name, eh?"

"When I used to come here, the café was owned by a guy named Hamish McTavish, who was every bit as Scottish as he sounds. When England were knocked out of the 2002 World Cup, by Brazil, he decked out the place in Scottish flags and tartan, and somebody put a brick through the window."

"Serves him right!"

A phone started ringing in a back room.

"Excuse me, would you?" Paddy said.

No sooner had Paddy disappeared than I became aware of a large presence looming over me and casting a shadow over the table. I looked up to see the duchess from breakfast time who had unnerved me with the intensity of her scrutiny. She was upright, in every sense of the word, and she looked not a little uptight too.

Had she been following me?

When she asked if she might join me, I told her to be my guest. I was intrigued. Was she an emissary of Providence come to give me the answers to all my questions? What was certain was that I had sparked her imagination into suggesting that I was somebody from her past, either a real person, flesh and blood, or else an ethereal throwback, an apparition, a spectral intimation of a long-lost loved-one. I knew that well enough for the simple reason that she looked as though she had seen a ghost.

"I thought you were …" she began.

"You thought I was who?"

The lady was dressed all in black (from coat, through ankle-length skirt, to boots); she reached into her black leather handbag and pulled out a black leather purse, from which she took a photograph which she placed on the table for me to study.

I picked up the photograph and beheld my younger self, only in black-and-white, and wearing clothes in which my younger self would not have been seen dead. It took me a few minutes to digest mentally what I was seeing.

"That could be *me*," I said, astonished.

"It's my late husband Anthony."

"He was a handsome young man."

"He was twenty when that photo was taken. I was eighteen at the time. We married a year later. He would be sixty-five now."

"I'm sorry for your loss."

My sorrow was genuine and for that she nodded her appreciation.

"My name's Andrea."

"Frankie…"

"You must think me rather morbid, walking around this town dressed for a funeral."

"It's funereal weather; and, anyway, look at me, dressed in black. I look like the Grim Reaper on his day off."

A period of silence ensued as we crumbled back into our separate days. I did not dwell on the photograph for long because the similarity between Anthony and me was so uncanny that I simply dismissed it as one of those coincidences that cannot be explained without recourse to the supernatural. I turned over the froth of my cappuccino with the spoon. I looked out of the window and beheld a windsurfer trying to save the life that he had recklessly put at risk by taking to the waves in the first place. As Paddy had said, there is always one. I looked across the table at my companion. Her face was hard to read. It bespoke both great happiness and profound sadness. I asked myself the question: whose face doesn't betray the gamut of emotions at sixty-three?

"Anthony and I called ourselves the 'A Team'."

"Because of your names?"

Andrea nodded. "We spent our honeymoon here. It was the year after the Queen's Silver Jubilee. The town was still decked out in bunting. This is the first time I've been back here since."

"I suppose back then people *did* come to places like Fleetpool for their honeymoons."

"At the time, we didn't have much money. Anthony's business was just getting off the ground. He made a great success of it. We both grew up in the worst part of Macclesfield. But even that's quite posh. We ended up living in Sale. Anthony left me a rich woman. But I would be happier if he were still alive, and we were living on the streets of Fleetpool."

The coincidences just kept coming.

"Why are you here, Frankie?"

"For reasons similar to yours . . . "

"You can tell me your story over dinner," she said. "It will be my treat."

"Well, I . . . "

"Shall we meet by the pier at seven o'clock this evening?"

"Sure," I replied as I grasped helplessly for one good reason to decline the invitation.

"Thank you," she said.

Paddy came back into the café just as Andrea was making to leave. He and I watched as she departed with a languid, sinuous grace that would have beguiled two blind men, negotiating even the rattling, shaking doors and vanishing into the wind and rain like a gilded vessel gliding serenely over a calamitous sea. Though she had made an impression on me, it would take some time for that impression fully to register. By the time we met that evening, I would have the measure of her. I would have to let the impression she made on me settle while I went about my business.

"Is she a friend of yours?" Paddy asked, still bound by Andrea's spell.

"I'm glad you, too, saw her," I replied, "because I wasn't sure that she was entirely real."

"She was real enough," Paddy said. "A fine figure of a woman."

"Enchanting . . . "

"Another cappuccino?"

"No, thanks, I need to get on."

I would arrive at the pier five minutes early for my date with Andrea, to find her already there, apparelled gloriously in a violet-coloured velvet dress, with black stilettoes and matching handbag.

We would dine at an Italian place, Mario's, one of the town's classier establishments, and we would talk for several hours. Andrea would remark that nobody gets to her age without regrets, to which, without meaning to be contentious, I would reply that I was nearly forty yet regretted nothing. I would ask Andrea what regrets she had. "Not making the most of my husband while he was alive," she would say. "Not being with him enough. I mean *really* being with him. It's more about the *quality* of the time than the *quantity*."

Andrea would give me more than enough to think about.

SIXTEEN

Guilt

Catholic theology posits four cardinal virtues: fortitude, patience, temperance and justice. These human qualities are so bound up together that somebody possessing any one of these virtues is bound to possess the other three too. Somebody with great forbearance and strength of character, for example, is unlikely to be impatient, intemperate and unjust. The four cardinal virtues bespeak honour, dignity and reliability. Anyone characterised by these four virtues is someone you can trust with your life.

I mention the four cardinal virtues, rather than, say, the three theological virtues—faith, hope and charity—because I wish to suggest a quartet of emotions as being similarly intrinsically connected. They are: guilt, remorse, regret and shame. Experience any one of these emotions and one is bound to experience, at once, each of the other three to a greater or lesser extent. Cheat someone and we feel guilty (for having violated some personal standard); we feel remorse (for having hurt the other, even if they are not aware that they have been cheated); we regret what we have done (we wish that we had not cheated the other); and we feel shame (for having betrayed a societal or other collective standard of behaviour).

Let us focus on guilt.

Guilt is a conflict with ourselves which demands to be resolved. It can fester, disabling us thereby. It can be denied, but only for so long.

I speak of *personal* guilt.

Personal guilt is so powerful an emotion—it can eat away at one's soul by stirring the conscience—that psychology, philosophy and religion, the three principal pillars of the intellect, have expended much time and energy thinking, talking and writing about it.

Psychologists connect guilt with notions of repression and projection.

In philosophy, the Epicureans' idea of guilt as being an emotion to be efficiently jettisoned the better to remain in a state of *ataraxia*, which pertains to a state of psychic equilibrium, is central, as is Nietzsche's concept of "bad conscience" as an agent of the enfeeblement of the Western mind, a debilitating condition for which he blames two millennia of Christian indoctrination.

Catholic guilt is what springs to mind when we think of religion and its interplay with the guilt complex.

The fulcrum of Catholic (and, more broadly, Christian) faith is the resurrection of Jesus Christ, for, as Saint Paul remarked, if Jesus did not rise from the dead then "our faith is in vain".

In Catholic theology (and practice), guilt is entwined with notions of trespass, debt, expiation and, crucially, sin (actions that offend Almighty God).

Pagan religions, too, carry the idea of sin (offences against any or all of the gods), but they insist that the debt for the offence must be paid by human beings, even by innocent human beings, through some kind of propitiation.

Catholics believe that God Himself (through His Only Begotten Son) paid mankind's debt of sin by sacrificing Himself on the cross, and that redemption comes through accepting Christ's sacrifice and by conforming oneself to God's sacrificial love by living according to God's revealed moral law.

The Catholic Mass begins with the Penitential Act, the centrepiece of which is the *Confiteor*. Here we have guilt as the Latin *culpa*, compounded in *maxima culpa* (great or grievous fault), occasioned by sins of both commission and omission.

In Catholicism, atonement is sought in the Sacrament of Reconciliation (which is sacramental confession), in which rite the penitent confesses to the priest (who acts *in persona Christi*) and, in exchange for an Act of Contrition and the fulfilment of due penance, is granted absolution for his sins (though punishment for the *consequences* of the confessed transgressions may remain outstanding).

I dwell on Catholic guilt because a friend of mine, in Sudbury, is a Catholic, and he (a member of the congregation of the Church of All Saints, which neighbours my pub) regularly exhorts me to forego any ideas of Catholic guilt as being in any way a negative thing. He insists—and I do not disagree with him—that guilt (of any kind, not just Catholic) can be constructive, for it can serve as an incentive to virtue.

Guilt, he asserts, can be a force that drives one to better one's character, thereby avoiding the alternatives: the guilt from which apathy, helplessness and hopelessness ensue; or the guilt that transports one into the realms of masochism and self-flagellation.

Guilt, then, can drive us to do our best, or it can devour us and so manifest the worst in us.

Like anyone else, I carry around with me my fair share of guilt.

That guilt forces me to ask questions of myself.

Did I love my father enough? Did I love him at all? Did I try hard enough to understand him?

Likewise, regarding my mother.

"Honour thy father and thy mother." How faithfully do I observe this the Fourth Commandment?

Do I work hard enough at the relationship with my brother?

Am I using my God-given talents properly?

Do I treat others as I would expect them to treat me? Do I do as I would be done by?

Have I always treated women with respect?

Did I take care of Leanne well enough? Should I have kept her in my life by not allowing her to drift away? Should I have been considering the possibility that she did not want me to find her?

Then there is Donna, around whom much of my guilt circles, like vultures over the remains of a half-devoured carcass.

Donna would be the last person to dissent from any claim that our marriage is largely one of convenience, though I have never been quite able to shake off the notion that I have cheated her by depriving her of her right to be with a man better suited to her, a man, indeed, who could have given her a child.

Yes, ours is the "perfectly serviceable relationship" of which my father spoke; and Donna herself never loses an opportunity to celebrate our union for being one characterised unashamedly by unsentimental mutual convenience and teamwork (my imagination buttressed by her business nous); and yet, still, I am unable to dismiss the idea that I benefit substantially more from our marriage than Donna.

Possibly because I am fundamentally an impractical person, I need to be surrounded by people possessed of a quiet, efficient knowhow, people like Johnny Watkins, Mrs Baxter, and Donna.

For me, such people are the grit in the oyster of life.

The world needs people like them.

I need people like them.

Though he comes but rarely to our pub, Irving is full of admiration for what Donna and I have done in turning it into one of the most popular watering holes in town. He often speaks of our "little goldmine" and the "fantastic job" that we have done. He knows that we have had some luck, but he knows also that we have, through ingenuity and foresight, made much of that luck for ourselves. Donna and I had been tenants of Marchmain Brewery for two years when the company informed us of its intention to sell the Cherry Tree Inn (so called because it had been built on the site of an old cherry orchard) to a property developer; we had been told that the deeds of the property allowed for it to remain as a public house, should the brewery ever be minded to sell, as long as a buyer could be found with a viable business plan to continue running the place as a licenced premises; accordingly, then, we had been given first refusal; somehow, we had come up with the money and the pub had been our home ever since (though we had ventured to change its name to the Riverside Tavern).

When we assumed ownership of the pub, at that time, pubs everywhere were metamorphosing into restaurants, or what were known as gastropubs; the trend was well established, and it had reached the stage where most public houses were restaurants first and pubs second. Our pub had bucked the trend, not because my wife and I were in possession of an excess of entrepreneurial flair, but because we saw a gap in the market for pubs without food, so we simply stayed where we were, commercially speaking. We were "old school" in our belief that the only solids that should be served in a pub were crisps and peanuts. Our conservatism had its roots in the traditional tastes of our regular customers, who would have voted with their feet had we started serving edible fare as unthreatening as pie and chips. We had innovated by staying the same. We had moved on by staying where we were. We had simply known our customers, who they were and what they liked, and we had attracted new customers thereby. So many businesses fail because they do not know their customers. Irving understands that all too well. As an accountant, he has wound up many a failed company; he has seen many a going concern turn into a gone concern; "too many by half", as he likes to say, such as Go Pizza, in North Street, which is now very much a case of Gone Pizza. "Someone always benefits from a crisis," my brother is also given to saying. Well, Donna and I had averted a crisis by remaining true to tradition, a principle to which would-be revolutionaries everywhere should pay heed.

I have used the third-person plural, when I ought to have used the third-person singular, since Donna was and is singularly the brains of our partnership, the one with the Midas touch when it comes to business.

She never puts a foot wrong in the world of commerce.

Do I love her for that?

If I do love her, it is a quiet, undemonstrative love born of admiration.

At the very least, what I feel for Donna is tremendous respect.

Mere respect, indeed.

All the same, I felt guilty about my pursuit of Leanne.

We carry so much guilt inside us.

We feel guilty about this, that, and the other.

We feel guilty about feeling guilty.

We feel guilty about *not* feeling guilty.

We are host to guilt heaped upon guilt.

"We travel with a corpse in the cargo."

So said Ibsen.

Well might we say that we travel with *corpses* in the cargo.

SEVENTEEN

Night & Day

My every day during that week of exploration in Fleetpool ended with a shower before bed, and that shower would perk me up sufficiently to suppress tiredness, leaving me wide awake as I climbed into bed and contemplated sleep.

I would send Donna a text message with the synopsis of my day, and we would exchange goodnights and assure each other of our mutual love.

I would feel a pang of guilt (how guilt would continue to harass me at every turn) about what I was doing, and how it must have been affecting Donna, and I would convince myself that I was simply doing what I had to do, and that Donna understood that.

I would ask myself if I deserved to have a wife as steadfast, loyal and uncomplaining as Donna, and answer that, no, I did not, but that, since our relationship was so solidly founded on trust, neither of us should ever dare to doubt the fidelity of the other.

Had either of us ever given the other reason to doubt our fidelity? No, we had not.

Would Donna expect recompense for damaged feelings occasioned by my treachery in seeking out Leanne? No, she would not, but that would not stop me from trying to make amends in some way. Nothing so crass as flowers or chocolates, a weekend away, perhaps, somewhere like Devon, a part of the country that Donna adored.

Anyway, I would tell myself at the end of each day, such considerations could wait.

It was not a case of my loving Donna less but of my loving Leanne more.

One night, as I prepared to sleep, I reached over to my travel bag on the chair by the bed and took out an old Nokia mobile phone, one of the first such devices to appear on the market around twenty years ago. It was the phone that Mrs Baxter had given me to keep in touch with her when I was out on the streets sleeping rough with Leanne. She had simply wanted to know where we were and that we were safe. Apart from that first time, when she found us sleeping in the bandstand, she had never come looking for us with a view to persuading us—or, rather, Leanne, since she was the one who had needed persuading—to return to the guest house. She had respected our space and allowed us to make our own decisions. Only when we were safely back under her roof did she ever suggest that Leanne consider seeking professional help for her troubles, help that she, Mrs Baxter, offered to facilitate.

Leanne had a recurring need to go walkabout, a compulsion that she herself could never explain.

It was a need that needed explaining.

The old phone had died on that August Bank Holiday Monday when I fished Leanne out of the sea at Splash Point. The phone had gone into the water with me and my clothes and my shoes. It had never recovered from its dip in the sea and had been unusable ever since. It had only ever had one number in its list of contacts, Mrs Baxter's, but that number had been inaccessible since my act of salvation, as if the sea had washed it away. The phone was with me now simply as a talisman. I hoped that it would not delay in working its magic.

Why had Leanne taken such a dreadful plunge? Without a doubt, something had triggered her inner desperation and left her so lacking in hope that she preferred being swallowed by the sea to another day in the land of the living, a land where she felt she would never belong. I had woken up in the middle of the night on that Monday, twenty years before, found her gone, feared the worst, and, panting heavily with a horrible sense of foreboding, gone out looking for her. In the deserted streets, I had heard her cries and mistaken them for an auditory hallucination. But they were real cries for help, all too real, and I had heeded them, gone to them, and leapt into the sea to still them. Even as I was saving her life, even as I was dragging her to the shore with all the strength I could summon, I feared that she would never forgive me for preserving her; that, despite the cries for help, she had wanted to die.

Perhaps that is why I wanted so badly to see her: to be forgiven.

I wanted to be forgiven for the greatest thing I had ever done.

Night came, as it always comes, day after day, but, as ever, it was never restful.

Running, dreamless sleep eluded me.

Oblivion was denied me.

There was only the fitful sleep broken by the nightmarish fear that Leanne, too, would elude me, and that she would be denied me; broken, too, by the pulsating excitement inherent in the realisation that finding Leanne again was my destiny, and that that was a script already written, indelibly etched in the annals of time.

The drama of the stormiest day is a mute beast beside the verbal pyrotechnics of the stillest of nights.

The night holds all the secrets of the day, but we must be at rest, oblivious, to receive them.

We begin each new day as hopelessly in the dark as we ended the previous day.

Day stands to life as night stands to death.

EIGHTEEN

Childhood

My days in Fleetpool, on my return visit, had one common feature, for every afternoon I would spend about an hour sitting on the promenade in a deckchair, taking in the view of the beach and the sea, out towards the horizon, the deckchair and I supporting each other in our attempts not to be blown away.

I hate deckchairs. I can never work out how to put them up or how to fold them back up once I have finished with them. The seats of deckchairs are always too close to the ground, and the synthetic fabric always generates so much static electricity that I often feel as though I am being slowly electrocuted. Getting myself up out of a deckchair is like pulling myself up off the ground, from a sitting position, whilst clutching some invisible handrail, a would-be mobility-aid for a fit young person. All in all, it is hard to credit how a thing designed to give one so much pleasure can be the source of so much discomfort, and I often wonder if other people are similarly afflicted, the tribulation not mine alone.

The deckchairs on the promenade had to be paid for and returned to the various little depots scattered round about, though some people were inclined to leave them exactly where they had pitched them, like abandoned tents of an army in retreat. I found one such deserted specimen, on the Wednesday afternoon, and lowered myself into it, delicately, taking care not to fall with such force that the fragile structure would collapse and swallow me whole; having effected the manoeuvre with due poise and dignity, my mind drifted back to the past, like the clouds floating westward across the horizon.

That is when the boy appeared.

He was dressed like a typical middle-class boy trying to keep warm in the chill of an English summer. He looked about ten years old.

He was standing beside me, gazing at me, imploringly, as if I had summoned him and he was awaiting instructions.

I was startled.

"Hello, young man," I said.

"Hello," he replied timidly.

"Can I help you?" It was a silly question.

"I just saw you, that's all." It was a strange answer.

"Are you alone?"

"I'm with my mum and dad."

"Where are they?"

"I don't know."

"Have you lost them?"

"I suppose so."

"Would you like me to help you find them?"

He shrugged his shoulders sadly.

"Are you hungry?"

He shrugged his shoulders again as he regarded me with pleading eyes. My heart ached for the boy, and I wanted to protect him from whatever horrors he was going through. I felt responsible for him, as if what I was about to say and do would affect him for the rest of his life.

"What's your name?"

"Peter . . ."

"Nice to meet you, Peter. My name's Frankie."

I invited him to grab himself a deckchair so that we could chat before I got us something to eat, but he said that he preferred to stand. He was not the easiest of boys to talk to. As we chatted aimlessly, I wondered how I was going to locate his parents and what I was going to say to them once I had found them. I was in a potentially compromising situation.

He told me that he lived in Graduate Heights, that he supported Fleetpool Town, and that his favourite player was Desmond Donnelly.

We were together for only ten minutes, but during that time I was his guardian.

"My mum and dad are always fighting," the boy confessed, "and, when they fight, they forget . . ."

"Forget what?" I asked.

"That I'm there . . ."

"I'm sorry to hear that, Peter."

"And they forget to feed me."

Now that he mentioned it, he did look somewhat undernourished, and I nearly wept at the boy's revelation.

"You should talk to someone about that," I said.

"I'm talking to *you*."

"Come on," I said as I got to my feet. "Let's go and get something to eat."

At that moment, the parents appeared.

"So," the father intoned with all the dramatic effect of an actor pronouncing the opening words of a play before an expectant audience, "there you are."

The mother was speechless, and she would remain so for the duration of the episode; she barely set eyes on her son; instead, she fixed her narrowed eyes on me, as if she were silently holding me to account for the commission of some great moral wrong.

On the surface, Peter's parents were the stereotypical suburban couple exuding affluence, assured of their place in the world, but from beneath the surface came some toxic energy, like poisonous gas seeping from the cracks in a rock.

The boy simply stood there, watching his parents with scared eyes.

Again, I was thrown into the role of the boy's guardian, but I felt powerless to help him.

The man turned his attention to me.

"Do we know you?" he asked, his accent refined but his tone threatening.

"I doubt it," I replied.

"Only, if we find our boy talking to a strange man, we're bound to wonder if we know the man."

"Your son came up to me and started talking to me."

"Is that so?"

"He told me that he'd lost his parents, and I said I'd help him find them, but you seem to have saved me the trouble."

"Our boy is a slippery character, always slipping away…"

"You might want to keep a closer eye on him in future."

"I'll be sure to keep your advice in mind."

With that the family of three was gone, though not without one more icy stare from the father, a lingering glare from the mother, and an imploring search from the eyes of the boy.

The episode was over almost before it began, and for a moment I was left wondering if it had happened at all. It had unsettled me so much that I needed something normal, something wholesome, to reset myself, so I bought myself a vanilla ice-cream, even though I had no appetite for it whatsoever.

I felt haunted by the family, and was made to reflect on parenthood and childhood, and how the failures of the former blight the latter, so that the world revolves in a perpetual cycle of needlessly inflicted trauma.

There was a group of four children on the beach, struggling to build a sandcastle with wet sand (since the tide was outgoing), and seeing them took me back to the hot afternoon, two decades ago, when Leanne and I had insinuated ourselves into a group of four children who were in a hurry to build a sandcastle to beat both the incoming tide and the storm that was brewing ominously overhead. The six of us had excitedly finished building the sandcastle just as the waves crashed in to knock it down and the heavens opened to send everyone on the beach scurrying for shelter like bees seeking the sanctuary of the hive.

If I had to say which was the happiest day of my time with Leanne, it would have to be that day, when we sought the fellowship of children, when we were little more than children ourselves.

Nobody got off the beach dry that day, but nobody cared about that, least of all Leanne and I, who were basking in the glow and the warmth of carefree days, endless days, sacred days, and a love upon which no worldly affairs could ever hope to intrude.

Our happiness was constrained by neither time nor place, it would endure beyond Fleetpool, going with us wherever we went, even if, God forbid, we should ever part; it would transport us to a place where no machine kept count, and where no umpire kept the score.

On that July day, as we fled the storm, we found refuge in Sea Place Café, and we drank our coffee soaked to the skin but without a care in the world.

"Frankie?"

After the disturbing encounter with Peter and his parents, seeing Trevor Peach was the perfect tonic. He was another one of mine and Leanne's erstwhile benefactors. He used to feed us at the soup kitchen that he ran for the homeless. He had become rich after selling his company at the ripe old age of thirty-five and had dedicated the rest of his life to running his charity. He was the type of man who would make a saint feel morally culpable. In his company, I had always felt grubby, shamed by his good works and selfless deeds, though he would have felt mortified had he known just how much of a shadow was cast by the brilliance of his halo.

He was ageing so well that he had barely changed in twenty years, as if virtue had made a pact with time and spared him the wrinkled, greying afflictions of his fellow mortals.

My conversation with Trevor was substantially the same as my conversations with Mehmed and Mrs Baxter had been that week. Back at his soup kitchen, he introduced me to some of his regular visitors, and I chatted with them whilst Trevor prepared some food.

There was Nelly Crawford, a perennially drunk old lady who shuffled around town with a bottle of liquor in each hand, her idea, perhaps, of a balanced diet.

There was Chris Needham, a Biggles-type character with a stammer and an encyclopaedic knowledge of World War Two aircraft.

There was Tommy Goodison, a veteran of the Falklands War who had fallen on hard times and who was bitter at the British state for the neglect of him and people like him.

There was a couple in their twenties who were living in a hostel whilst waiting for a council flat to be allocated to them. Love confers limitless possibilities, and they, though not in a good place at that moment in time, had time and, I hoped with all my heart, fortune on their side.

As he was showing me the foodbank that he had set up adjacent to the soup kitchen, he became quite emotional, so that for a moment I ceased to recognise my phlegmatic old friend.

"It's so good to see you, Frankie," he stammered, almost cried. "I thought I saw you on the seafront yesterday, but I said to myself, no, it can't possibly be Frankie."

"I guess it *was* me."

"You know something, Frankie," he went on, "I do this because somebody has to do it, and that somebody might as well be me, but it shouldn't be like this, and it wouldn't be like this if people took better care of each other."

"It all starts in the home, Trevor," I said. "If it goes wrong there, it's hard to put right later on."

"That's so true, Frankie," he said. "You know, several times a week a boy comes here, to the soup kitchen, for something to eat. He's about ten years old. He comes after school.

He's a nice kid, with impeccable manners, well-dressed and well-spoken. He's evidently from a pretty well-off family. Why he comes here, I don't know."

"Because he's hungry?"

"Oh, yes, but why should he be hungry when he's obviously from a good family?"

"A wealthy family is not necessarily a good family."

"From what I can make out," Trevor replied, "the boy's barely fed at home."

"What's the boy's name, Trevor?"

"Peter," Trevor said. "His name is Peter."

NINETEEN

Hebden Bridge

On the Friday morning of that week, I informed Nadine of my plans: that I was heading for Hebden Bridge (and who knew where else from there), but that I would be back in Fleetpool and the Marine Gardens Hotel no later than Sunday evening.

I did not check out of the hotel, but continued to pay for the room, mine and Leanne's room, room sixteen.

Via Blackpool, Preston, Blackburn, Burnley and Todmorden, I arrived in Hebden Bridge, at midday, and booked myself a room for one night in the Bridgehead Hotel, a capacious, castle-like lodging overlooking the Rochdale Canal.

After dropping my baggage in the room, I took lunch in the hotel restaurant, which was so busy with what appeared to be tourists that I thanked my lucky stars for having been able to obtain a room in the place at all, and I wondered what was so special about Hebden Bridge that so many people had come to see it.

Over lunch (shepherd's pie and a pint of Yorkshire ale), a Chekhovian moment overtook me, though it was simply three women who sprang to my mind, rather than three sisters.

For no reason other than that my brain had little else to occupy it, since I had shelved any thoughts as to how exactly I was going to find out the slightest thing about Leanne in such a chaotic place, a situation in which I felt utterly anonymous and helpless, I began thinking about Leanne, Donna and Nadine.

I compared them. I contrasted them.

In my mind, then, I drew a Venn diagram of the three women and looked for those shaded areas denoting an overlap of shared characteristics, and for the darkest area where all three intersected.

There were similarities between Leanne and Nadine in terms of their foxy attitude to the world, which found expression in a punchy irreverence, though Leanne's forthright demeanour stemmed from insecurity, fear, and vulnerability, whereas Nadine's emanated from total assurance of self, her place in the world, where she was and where she was going.

Leanne and Donna converged temperamentally in their essential reticence, in their tendency not to speak until spoken to, and in their proneness to fall into bouts of introspective silence. In this regard, I had the impression that Nadine would happily talk for the duration of a flight between London and Sydney.

Between Donna and Nadine there was a shared ability to plan ahead to realise their goals with a minimum of fuss and a maximum of efficiency.

What connected all three women?

Knowing what I knew about the three women—which, I had to concede, was far from everything—I could discern no common attribute other than shoulder-length black hair. That was it. They had only this basic physical characteristic in common. That was enough, however, for the resemblances to be uncanny, even a touch spooky.

I had even toyed with the idea that both Donna and Nadine were doppelgangers of Leanne.

Thanks to Tommy from the Queen's Arms, in Fleetpool, I was in Hebden Bridge, a charming place about which I knew little.

What *did* I know about Hebden Bridge?

That it was situated in the Upper Calder Valley.

That it had become a colony of artists, hippies and yuppies.

That it had become a commuter town for people desirous of a congenial habitat away from the dirty, smelly places where they worked.

That, owing to the topography of the town, Hebden Bridge was host to many a tenement building, great towers in the hills that somehow put me in mind of Edinburgh.

That the Rochdale Canal (connecting Sowerby Bridge and Manchester) was a notable feature of the town.

Perhaps that was quite a lot to know about a small settlement in the heart of old industrial England.

On reflection, I knew as much about Hebden Bridge as I needed to know, and, possibly, more.

In the afternoon, I took a stroll along the canal, and, as afternoon faded into evening, I looked around the town centre, which was charming, and was captivated by the Picture House which, I surmised, was as much a magnet for the cultural elite of the town as the Quay Theatre was for the intelligentsia of Sudbury.

I had a light dinner of lasagne (and the mandatory pint of Yorkshire ale) in a delightful pub named the Shoulder of Mutton. I placed myself in a corner and tried not to look sheepish.

It was there that I met yet another damsel with black hair, though this time the hair was much longer.

Was Providence again by my side, even as doppelgangers stalked me relentlessly?

She had been staring at me for several minutes, from the other side of the lounge bar, before she came over and sat with me.

She was about twenty-two years old and strikingly attractive, with dark hair cascading down her back like waters of ebony in freefall.

Her accent was more Harrogate than Hebden Bridge.

"I noticed you in the hotel restaurant earlier," she told me from across the table.

"I was the only person in the restaurant eating alone," I replied, "so I suppose I stood out like a sore thumb."

The young lady's eyes bespoke melancholy and a cynicism that belied her youth.

"I'm Sonia."

"And I'm Frankie."

"Since I'm alone, too, I thought we could talk."

"What would you like to talk about?"

"My boyfriend . . ."

It was a strange topic of conversation for a lonely young woman to broach with an older man, and a stranger to boot. I was intrigued.

"Okay," I said.

"I'm in a delicate situation, you see, I need advice, and you seem—oh, I don't know—sympathetic. You have a kind face."

"I hope I can help."

"My mum and dad own the Bridgehead Hotel. They're the most reactionary people you'll ever meet: three steps to the right of Genghis Khan, the pair of them. Next week, on Wednesday, my boyfriend comes out of prison. He's done three years for grievous bodily harm. My parents weren't fond of him before he smashed up two guys, because he's not 'our sort', he's an 'oik from Huddersfield', and they're using the GBH thing as, if you like, further evidence that he's nowhere near right for me."

"Why did he beat up the two guys?"

"He was defending my honour."

"That's all right then," I said with a suggestion of sarcasm.

Sonia detected the undertone of sarcasm and assured me that her Dale was *not* a violent man.

"You know him better than I do," I conceded.

"One night, in the saloon bar of the hotel, two guys started chatting me up when Dale was in the toilet. When he came out, he told the two guys to back off. One of them replied: 'She's not our type, anyway, mate. She's got no tits.' He was drunk but there was nothing wrong with his eyes. Dale went mad. He pummelled the pair of them—though, to be fair, one of them hadn't really said much—and ended up throwing one of them, the mouthy one, into a fruit machine and the other one over the bar and into the fridge door. They both left the hotel in the same ambulance."

"Like you said, he *was* defending your honour, though, perhaps, a tad overzealously."

"That's what my parents said. That's what the *judge* said."

"So, I'm guessing that you're wondering whether you should take Dale back?"

Sonia nodded.

"Has Dale given you any choice in the matter?"

"Oh, yes, he's been perfectly understanding. He told me that he'd understand if I wanted to move on."

"Do you?"

"Not really …"

"Do you love him?"

"Yes, but it's complicated, what with my parents and, well, I did visit him once a month at Wakefield Prison, so he's kind of expecting me to be there for him when he comes out."

"Will you be?"

"I won't be waiting for him outside the prison gate on Wednesday morning, but I'll be *here*."

"You have to decide if his volatility is something you can live with."

"He's not volatile. He just snapped with those two men. It was a one-off."

"If he's done it once, he can do it again."

"Dale's solid. He has good values. Even my parents would admit that. They're just snobs, because of his background."

"Based upon what you've told me, I'd say that he's worth a second chance."

"That's what I hoped you'd say."

"I wish you the best of luck."

Sonia offered to buy me a drink and, after some haggling about which one of us should have been buying the new round of refreshments, she went to the bar to fetch us both a drink. She returned with a pint of bitter for me and a bottle of

Stella Artois for herself. We talked about me and my reasons for being in Hebden Bridge and for staying at the Bridgehead Hotel. She was enchanted by my story and was adamant that I was doing nothing wrong in going after Leanne, since I was being honest with my wife, keeping nothing from her. We were engaged in an uplifting exercise in mutual affirmation, for which there was an abundance of mutual appreciation.

I attract loners, I suppose because I am a loner myself. Sonia had about her an aura of solitariness, which acted almost as an unspoken plea for solitude, as if she were happily cocooned in her own selfhood, wrapped in the enigma that she was. I considered her eminently worthy of a portrait. I resolved to make her my next subject. I did not need her to model for me, nor did I need a photograph of her, for I had already divined her essence, and that was all I needed. The theme of the portrait—for even portraits must have a theme—would be solitariness, that congenial loneliness that forswears lonesomeness as company, that spiritual quality that denotes separation and separateness from the ever-clamorous world.

In the depths of my contemplation of Sonia, she startled me with an announcement.

"I can help you find Leanne."

"You can?" Again, I found myself trying to contain my feverish excitement.

"I'm in charge of the hotel this evening, from seven o'clock. My parents have to go out—some corporate function or other—and Dave, our hotel manager, is at his mother's funeral, so I'm left running the place. I'll dig out Leanne's file from our personnel records. It will say where she went after she left here."

"I'm conscious that, as I look for Leanne, I'm dependent on people being prepared to break the rules."

"I'm happy to *bend* the rules for you."

If Sonia was only bending the rules, she was surely bending them to breaking point.

"I can't thank you enough," I said.

"You can thank me by buying me a drink in the bar later this evening."

"That's the least I can do."

"It's more than enough."

TWENTY

Whitby

It was the thirteenth day of August and Whitby was coated in a mist thick enough for one standing on the West Pier of the harbour not to be able to see clearly the East Pier across the water.

I had checked into the Harbour Hotel and was now standing in front of the abbey, the erstwhile Benedictine monastery, looking down on the mist-shrouded harbour below. Though it was nearly midday, the mist was stubbornly resisting all calls to disperse and be gone.

I had spent a few minutes in the cemetery of the adjacent church, Saint Mary's, Anglican, and was taking in the view. It was my first time in Whitby, and I was keen to see the abbey from the ground, at night, illuminated, though even in daylight I was getting a sense of how Bram Stoker was inspired by Whitby's ambience to transport his Transylvanian antihero, Count Dracula, to this quaint little fishing town on the coast of North Yorkshire.

Sonia had informed me that Leanne had worked in the Bridgehead Hotel, in Hebden Bridge, from the spring of 2003 to the autumn of 2007, whereupon she had moved to Whitby and the Harbour Hotel.

These periods were so long ago that I dared not entertain the notion that she might be still residing and working in these places.

What had Leanne done with herself in the period between our parting and the spring of the following year? I supposed that she had been resting, convalescing, under some form of rehabilitation. I asked myself where Leanne was during this time; and why she had disappeared off the radar for those—Mrs Baxter, principally—who might have helped her get back on her feet after the incident at Splash Point.

These questions were academic, not strictly pertinent to my investigation, my interrogation of time, in my quest to find Leanne; and, even if I were to find her, they would remain mere details, the draughtsman's embellishment of the artist's broad sweep across the canvas.

"Beautiful, isn't it?"

I was starting to wish that people would quit startling me with their sudden appearances out of nowhere. Wherever I went, a figure would emerge, materialise, take shape, arise, or otherwise come into being, from some unseen place. Given how frequently these irruptions occurred, I should never have found myself unsuspecting. It should have come as no surprise to me, then, that a man should make substance of himself out of mist and take his place beside me. Still less should I have been surprised that he should engage with me as if we were longstanding friends.

I looked right and beheld a man in a black raincoat and matching trilby. He was essentially smart, though embarked on a downward curve towards shabbiness. Give it another year, I thought, and people will be throwing money at him out of charity. His sort does not need to beg or sing or perform tricks for money, I mused, they need only stand or sit still and the money will come. I chided myself for making such a judgement, even as I excused myself for the judgement's having come involuntarily.

"I wouldn't know," I replied in jocular fashion. "I can't see it."

"Trust me, it's beautiful."

"If I stand here long enough," I said, "the mist will clear."

"Some people read about Whitby's windswept headland, dramatic abbey ruins, the church and its swooping bats, and the quaint maritime beauty of the harbour—all these tour-guide clichés—and, of course, they come here to see it all," the man went on. "Many people come here to live the whole *Dracula* experience."

"Coincidentally, I read *Dracula* earlier this year," I returned. "It's one of those books that you feel you ought to read, even if you don't really want to read it."

"Some of the tourists we get here think that Dracula was real, that he lived here, and that he's buried in this here churchyard. They're extremely disappointed when they learn that he's nothing more than a work of fiction."

"People write to characters in soap operas warning them that their spouses are having an affair, or warning them about some impending danger, thinking that the characters are real people."

"Yes," the man laughed, "well might Trigger in *Only Fools* have wondered why Gandhi made only one film before disappearing into obscurity."

I chuckled myself as I recalled that famous scene.

"My name's Harry Dunbar."

"Frankie McDowell…"

We pressed the flesh, though he pressed considerably harder than I.

"I've been coming up here every day for twenty years, in all weathers, you know, to admire the view. I'm fifty-seven now. Getting up here doesn't get any easier."

"You climb those steps?"

"Yes, those famous one-hundred-and-ninety-nine steps…"

"I counted one-hundred-and-ninety-eight steps on the way up."

"And you shall count two-hundred steps on the way down."

"How do you know that?"

"Because I, too, count one-hundred-and-ninety-eight steps on the way up, and two-hundred steps on the way down, every single time."

"Either you can't count or there's something supernatural going on."

"This being Whitby, I'd put my money on the latter."

"What's your line of work, Harry?"

"Look at me," he replied. "If I weren't an artist, what the hell else would I be doing?"

"Snap!"

"I thought I recognised a kindred spirit."

"I also own a pub."

"You're my kind of man twice over."

"I used to paint commonplace landscapes and portraits, but now my work is more abstract," I explained. "I produce fewer paintings than I used to, but they sell for more."

"I'm just a 'commonplace landscape' man myself," Harry said, so that I wondered if I had not offended him, "and there's enough to see in Whitby, and in Yorkshire, generally, to keep a jobbing artist going for a lifetime."

"I stayed overnight in Hebden Bridge before coming here," I said, "and I crossed the North York Moors, stopping for a break in Goathland."

Harry nodded knowingly and told me that he had spent the previous day in Sandsend, sketching, in preparation for his next batch of paintings. He then asked me where I was from.

"Sudbury, in Suffolk," I said.

"Ah, Constable country!" Harry exclaimed.

"Gainsborough, too," I said. "He was born in Sudbury. There's a statue of him on the Market Hill, but louts keep tipping paint over it, too stupid, I suspect, to appreciate the irony."

"What brings you to Whitby?"

I had no idea where to start answering that question, because it was too long a story, the beginning too far removed from the indeterminate end, so I offered Harry simply a two-word synopsis: "A woman."

"I might have guessed," he replied.

"I know that she was here, a few years ago," I said, "but I've no idea where she went afterwards."

"She might still be here."

"I doubt it."

"Why was she here?"

"She was working at the Harbour Hotel."

"What's her name?"

"Leanne Kenyon…"

"Well, she's definitely not there now."

"How do you know?"

"Because the long-term owner of the hotel, Jenny McRae, is, for want of a better word, my girlfriend. There's no Leanne Kenyon working there now, but then Jenny and I have only been an item for a couple of years, so I can't tell you how long ago Leanne left the hotel, or where she went after she left, but I can find out for you."

"I would be immensely grateful," I said as I thanked Providence for yet another good turn, though the pessimist in me was starting to feel like the jockey on a horse way out in front in the Grand National, with victory in sight, but fearful of coming a cropper at the final fence. It might be, I thought, that I would get so close to finding Leanne but run into a wall at the business end of my pursuit. That would be forever too tough a setback to endure.

"We artists must stick together," Harry declared with a winsome smile. "Leave it to me. I'll find out for you."

"Once again, I'm extremely grateful."

"Think nothing of it. You look like a decent sort. You obviously have good reason for wanting to find this woman, and that's entirely your business, of course."

"It's a long story," I said, "but I would be happy to tell it over a beer."

"Sounds good to me," Harry said. "I'm due at the hotel for lunch. In the meantime, why don't we grab a quick drink somewhere and you can tell me all about this Leanne."

"I'd be delighted."

Sure enough, on the way down to the harbour, Harry and I counted two-hundred steps, and we discussed this (apparent) supernatural discrepancy, and much else besides, over a couple of jars in the Quayside Tavern, the pub next-door to the hotel, directly opposite the marina.

Jenny, Harry told me, had converted her attic for Harry to use as a studio, and he enjoyed painting by the bay window which gave him an abundance of natural light and a gorgeous view of the harbour, the sea, and the abbey on top of the cliff away to the right. That afternoon, he would take me to his studio and show me the paintings of his that he was waiting to sell, and I would tell him, perfectly sincerely, without any attempt at flattery, that he was selling himself short in describing himself as a "jobbing" painter. His work was considerably better than that, and I had no hesitation in paying him five-hundred pounds for his oil-on-canvas evocation of Whitby Abbey, lit up at night, as seen from the marina.

As I ate lunch in the hotel restaurant, I overheard Harry and Jenny talking at the bar, Harry's having steered the conversation deftly onto the subject of Leanne.

"I met a strange bloke in town this morning, a Scotsman," Harry began. "He didn't show me any ID, and I didn't ask to see any, but I think he was a private detective."

"Why do you think that?"

"He wanted some information, and, for some reason, he thought he could get it from me."

"What did he want to know?"

"He asked me if I knew a Leanne Kenyon."

"What did you tell him?"

"I told him that the name rang a bell but that I couldn't place her."

"She used to work here, but that was long before we met."

"It was just a bizarre coincidence, then, that he should ask me."

"Quite!"

"How long did the girl work here?"

"She was hardly a girl. She was about twenty-five when she came here. She stayed three years or so. Lovely lass, she was. She went to work at the Beach Hotel, in Scarborough. She got a good job as a restaurant manager."

I calculated that Leanne left Whitby about twelve years ago, which made it unlikely that she would still be in Scarborough: she was not the sort to let the grass grow under her feet, ever restless as she was.

Harry had just given a masterclass in luring someone into a trap and, by catching them off-guard, eliciting a revelation that discretion might have forestalled.

In falling into Harry's trap, Jenny had sent me on my way to Scarborough. I would go early the following morning. I was on Leanne's trail. I was closing in on her. I could feel myself getting closer and closer to her, drawn to her, inexorably, as Providence matched me with its hour.

I had only one day left, but that would be enough. I was sure of that.

During the afternoon, I wandered around the town and the harbour, imbibing the *genius loci*, an unconscious process that would, as always, feed my imagination and so enrich the seams of creativity that I could not help but mine. How many paintings would this profoundly atmospheric place inspire? It was impossible to say. All my subsequent works, perhaps, though, more likely, only parts of all of them, and indeterminate parts at that.

Where does creativity come from? That was the question upon which I meditated as I leaned against an iron railing on the harbour, facing the marina, with the abbey looking down upon me with its benignant eyes, seemingly imploring me to produce an answer.

Creativity is all that the artist has experienced, knowingly or otherwise, the sensory data that he mines not confined to the five senses of the physical realm alone.

Many books have been written on this very subject, though, I would submit, by people who are not creative themselves, at least not in the artistic sense. Freud, for example, penned a short study of Leonardo da Vinci, a book that is all the more brilliantly lucid for its brevity, and which delves into the depths, and explores the labyrinths, of a near-impenetrable mind.

Well might the artist meditate on the phenomenon of creativity, his own and creativity in general, but it is not the job of the artist to *explain* it; indeed, if he were to do so, that would serve only to stymie his creativity, in the same way that, if one were to meditate on the mechanics of, say, walking, a simple task for an able-bodied person, one might find oneself struggling to put one foot in front of the other.

I was Harry's guest for dinner, which was taken at one of Whitby's finest fish-and-chip restaurants, after which we proceeded to one of Whitby's finest pubs, where, with my early start the following morning in mind, I restricted myself to two pints of ale.

To express my gratitude, for his help in garnering the information that I needed, I bought the drinks. We talked nothing but art, and I invited him to Suffolk, promising that I would take him to Southwold, where my artistic career had begun. We talked about Yorkshire and its power to inspire artists; and we discussed Whitby, Southwold, and other places where artists are known to go to indulge their common passion, places such as Saint Ives, the Lake District, and, yes, Hebden Bridge.

I retired to bed with thoughts of Count Dracula and the book that I had read earlier that year. I had forgotten many of the details, but the sensibility of the book still permeated my being somehow, and Whitby had stirred it.

Before sleep, I looked out of the window and beheld the abbey, a lamp aglow and not hidden under any bushel.

For its power to inspire great art, I was in the shadow of greatness itself.

TWENTY-ONE

Scarborough

Scarborough, to my great surprise, was magnificent, vibrant where Whitby had been sedate, expansive where Whitby had been cloistered and constrained, and glamorous where Whitby had been silent and brooding.

Such were the contrasts.

There were similarities too.

Both towns had literary associations, Anne Brontë being Scarborough's. The author of *The Tenant of Wildfell Hall* is buried in Saint Mary's Church, in Scarborough, and on that Sunday afternoon, as I toured the castle, I made sure to visit the grave of the gifted writer who was part of a trio of gifted writers, and a sorority, too, no less.

Saint Mary's Church, for the nomenclature, was another correspondence registered.

Both towns had a harbour, a West Pier and an East Pier, and a headland regally displaying a famous landmark (the castle, in the case of Scarborough).

The fishing industry was a feature of both towns.

According to Scarborough's own version of magnificence (vibrancy, expansiveness, and glamour), the Grand Hotel, atop Saint Nicholas Cliff, was typical, and Whitby (not that it would mind) had nothing at all to match it. It overlooks the South Bay like a colossus, a multitiered monster of a building pulsating with human life.

The Grand Hotel is built upon a theme, time, for it has four towers (representing the seasons), twelve floors (the months of the year), fifty-two chimneys (the weeks of the year), and three-hundred-and-sixty-five bedrooms (the days of the year).

The weather—warm and sunny—accentuated the radiant golden colour of the hotel's exterior, and it brought the town, always lively, to the full bloom of its summer life.

On the fourteenth day of August, I was lucky to be in Scarborough on one of its finest days of that year.

The Grand Hotel worked its charm on me so beguilingly that I was seduced into booking a room for the night therein, and I was given a chamber on the first floor of the upper tier so sumptuous—what with its giving onto a spacious terrace with a splendid view of the bay—that I was made to feel guilty for having indulged myself so shamelessly.

The Beach Hotel was nestled in the calmer confines of the North Bay, and it was there that I ventured to take dinner, confident that a few choice words with the right people would point the way on that, the final, leg of my journey towards my cherished reunion with Leanne.

How did I feel at what was very much the eleventh hour (and some) of my quest to find Leanne?

I was in a zone of serenity, overcome as I was with a quiet conviction that Providence would not let me down.

That Providence would fail me was simply out of the question.

I would not be denied at the death.

I had company for dinner, for a man of about my age planted himself opposite me and proceeded to talk to me as I ate. He looked shabby in a crumpled suit. His obtrusion was so subtle that I can barely remember how it happened, for one minute he was not there and the next minute he was, having, apparently, drifted into my space like smoke from some distant fire.

We might have exchanged pleasantries before he launched himself into a monologue. He might even have told me his name. I cannot remember.

I can remember plenty enough of what he told me because it was curiously compelling.

Having given me some facts about himself (details that I cannot recall), he went on to say that these facts were but details which, together, formed what society called his identity.

"I have no need for such things, such totems of meaning, such shibboleths of the modern world, and I'm not sure that I have much need for society either. Which is not to say that I dislike people, only that I have a horror of membership, the most pernicious form of which is the family."

His diction was unusually mechanical and robotic, his delivery deadpan, and yet he decorated his speech with striking metaphors.

"Who was my father?" he went on. "Who is my mother? That's assuming that she's still alive. Where is he in death and she in life? My father is dead, my mother merely absent, and has been since I was eight years old.

"My sister is simply remote, though she lives five miles up the road. She might as well be dead for all the life that's in her. She works in a perfume factory, and she thinks it's the best job in the world because she gets free perfume as a perk of the job. It's not even good perfume. She walks around smelling as though she's been doused in bleach, and cheap bleach at that. Her husband pours cheap aftershave over himself and spends most of every day stretched out on the sofa like a beached whale. Her son can never tear himself away from his computer games, and her daughter is a teenaged version of herself, bound to grow up and become her mother.

"My extended family are out there, somewhere, making no noise but always threatening to close in on me; they encircle me, poised to start making that circle smaller, an ever-decreasing circle, indeed. I wouldn't recognise any of them if my life depended on it. If they think nothing of me, I think of them still less.

"It gives me no pleasure to say any of this. It's just how it is: more facts.

"I talked about membership earlier. What kind of membership does marriage bestow upon me? Marriage is to me what a black eye is to a punch in the face: a simple consequence of what came before. That doesn't prevent me from respecting my wife. It would be hard not to admire such a strong and venerable woman. Why would I, her husband, be the only person in the world not to notice and appreciate the great cluster of virtues which, together, make up her character? She is more than a glimmer of hope in a dismal world. She gives me much. What I give her is not for me to say. My sense is that something worthwhile flows between us, like the two-way flow of traffic between two great cities. If it's not love then it's our own version of it, our attempt at embodying an ideal that can be conceived only at the expense of being able to find true fulfilment through it, by it, and in it.

"To anyone who would exhort me—implore me even—to love my wife, I would reply that if love is a word, and great love a celebrated speech, then what my wife and I share is but a whisper, a whispered word, perhaps, though, conceivably, something more abundant: the whisper of a brilliant speech.

"Love, indeed, is a chimera. It might be thought of as a giant cube, which is solid and predictable when seen from a distance, but, when viewed at close quarters, becomes the object of a lost perspective; something which can be touched but which cannot be entered into.

"I've been married ten years, and in that time I've succumbed to happiness of a kind, or at least contentment, fulfilment being a state of mind that I dare not contemplate. My wife and I are good together; we are, I dare say, the best thing that's ever happened to each other; but only to the extent that together we are productive, efficient, making the practicalities of life fall into place and work for our mutual benefit. We are not worth a single word of a romantic poet's lexicon. We are not Plato's *Symposium*, or Shakespeare's *Romeo and Juliet*, or even Wagner's *Tannhäuser*. We are the County Council's Information Technology Department's internal instruction manual for the newly implemented accounting system. There is a place for such a thing. It's called the world at large. It's the very thing that makes the world go round. It's nothing special, I grant you, but it gets the job done. Indeed, it's *because* it's nothing special that it *does* get the job done."

As I sat at the table, eating and listening to the man's epic monologue, I reflected that, with Leanne, I *had* experienced something special. Even so, I was mindful that the way I felt about Leanne was a projection of the ever-unfolding present onto the past, for what we experience at any given time is never what it becomes once that time has faded into the past and we start looking back at it with a mind's eye distorted by the ever-implacable demands of the present.

So much for the rationale: it was not enough to change what I felt for Leanne, which was love, true love, unchanging, unchangeable, eternal love.

No rationale could ever change that.

"Please forgive the intrusion," the man said, having appeared to realise, suddenly, as if someone had just slapped him in the face and woke him from a trance, that he had imposed upon me inexcusably.

"It's not a problem," I replied. "I'm sympathetic to what you say."

"You think me a tad cynical, perhaps?"

"All I would say, by way of criticism, is that you should cherish your wife. Do that at least."

"Oh, I *do* cherish her, in my own strange way."

"That's all right then," I said.

"I'm just such a dreadful misfit," the man said. "Are you familiar with the works of Flannery O'Connor?"

"Yes, I'm a fan of her work."

"Have you read *A Good Man Is Hard to Find*?"

"Yes, it's her best short story by a long way."

"Well, that's me, the Misfit, with a capital M."

"I doubt that you're the type to wipe out a family with a shotgun."

"No, but you get what I'm saying?"

"I do," I replied with exaggerated earnestness, just in case he *was* the type.

"I'm such a misfit that it's a miracle that I found someone prepared to marry me."

"All the more reason for cherishing your wife."

"You know, I was kicked out of university for something I didn't do."

"A miscarriage of justice?"

"Not exactly. Well, yes, perhaps. I studied history at university. Halfway through my second year, in a seminar, one of my teachers accused me of being so right-wing—I'm not remotely right-wing, by the way—that I was probably one of those Holocaust-deniers. To that, I replied: 'Which holocaust?' I wasn't denying any holocaust. I was simply asking him to which holocaust he was referring. The entire history of humanity is one big holocaust. There are holocausts going on as we speak."

"Well, there's *the* Holocaust, and there are all the other holocausts," I submitted.

"But we don't call 'all the other holocausts' holocausts, do we?"

"We often talk about Robespierre's Great Terror as if it's the only Terror that's ever been unleashed."

"That was my point. I returned an insult with a demand for academic rigour, for which I was expelled from the university on the grounds that I had denied the Holocaust."

"Since you said '*which* holocaust', rather than '*what* holocaust', I would say that you were harshly treated." I was flailing somewhat at this point, unable to find the right stance and tone: to agree with him on the points of academic rigour and freedom of speech, but without wishing to be seen as being remotely sympathetic to the goals of the perpetrators of the greatest crime in human history. "Did you appeal?"

"What good would that have done?"

"It would have cleared your name."

"I would have been hung out to dry. They didn't want me there. I asked too many awkward questions. They were looking for a reason to send me down, and I gave them one."

"Sometimes, you just have to play the game. You have to pick and choose your battles in life. Otherwise, you find yourself permanently at odds with the world."

"I'm finding it increasingly hard to communicate with people in the modern world. People aren't rational. There's something missing in their brains. They are all about prejudice, emotion, and they cling to received ideas unthinkingly."

"That's because the West today has moved on from the moral foundations of religious faith, and the rationalist principles of the Enlightenment, and put nothing in their places."

"That's exactly it! I knew you were a kindred spirit the moment I first saw you!" My companion was so animated that his eyes lit up, as if an electric switch somewhere had activated two lightbulbs inside his head. "That's why I had no hesitation in planting myself opposite you and holding forth."

I had finished my dinner of beef stew and dumplings and was now giving some attention to my beer. I would soon have to give some attention to my quest for information about Leanne.

"I've enjoyed chatting with you," I said.

"Are you on business here in Scarborough?"

"Not exactly," I replied. "I'm looking for someone."

"Are you a private detective?"

"No," I said, "it's personal."

"Is the person you're looking for from this area?"

"She worked at this hotel some years ago, as the restaurant manager, here, I suppose, in this very restaurant."

"What's her name?"

"Leanne Kenyon…"

"I don't know the name," the man declared, "but I know someone who will."

"Really?"

"Fiona Parker is the administrator here. She's married to the hotel owner's brother, but she's having an affair with my sister's husband's brother. It's the most unlikely liaison, but there you are. Anyway, I'm the only person—other than Fiona and her lover, of course—who knows about the affair. I could use that as leverage to get the information you need."

"Well, I wouldn't want…"

"I can tell that you're an honourable man, and that you have moral qualms about my suggestion, so here's what we do. I go into Fiona's office now. I tell her about you. If she's prepared to give me the information you need, or to give it to you, I don't mention the affair and what might happen were I to spill the beans. If the information isn't forthcoming then I use my leverage."

"It's not ideal," I said, "but it might be my best chance."

"Give me five minutes," the man said, and, with that, he was gone.

He was gone for just those five minutes, but that gave me ample time to reflect.

Notwithstanding the melancholy that was my prevailing mood throughout my return visit to Fleetpool, the experience, overall, had been a happy one. I had reconnected with the happiest time of my life, met old friends, made new friends, wallowed shamelessly in nostalgia, and cruised serenely on a sea of optimism.

There were only two blots on the experiential copybook.

The first was the encounter with Peter and his parents. That left the sourest of tastes in my mouth and had me wondering if I had not just looked into the eyes of evil. It was as if some terrible incident had marred an otherwise splendid holiday, in a place where the terrible had no right to be.

The other was this unscheduled meeting with this peculiar man.

It had simply not occurred to me that I would have to resort to devious means to elicit information about Leanne; mischievous means, perhaps, a ruse here and there, but nothing devious; and I felt only slightly less ashamed of having been *party* to dishonourable machinations as opposed to being the sole perpetrator thereof.

Anyway, the upshot was that I was potentially at the final hurdle, for Intuition was whispering in my ear and assuring me that there would be no more fences in the race; that the course was as good as run.

I was overcome with a frisson of excitement, my response to which was to buy myself another beer.

So, I thought to myself, this is where Leanne had plied her trade as a restaurant manager? She had dragged herself out of the quagmire of misery and despair, given herself a foothold in life, and found her balance, before taking slow and deliberate steps towards a respectable position in society.

How much help had she needed to achieve this remarkable feat, what kind of help had it been, and from whom?

These were the questions that I had barely asked myself before.

There was one question that I dared not ask myself, out of fear of the answer, mainly, but also because it was a question that would answer itself, were I to find Leanne.

Leanne's spirit pervaded the restaurant, permeating every chair, every table, the bar, the floor, the ceiling, all of it, without exception.

As Intuition whispered in one ear, Leanne's gentle words caressed the other: "Tomorrow, my love, we will be together."

I wiped tears from my eyes with a napkin, an accessory that seemed not to mind not being used for its intended purpose.

"Fiona Parker will see you now."

The man was back, having again stepped out of some parallel dimension and obtruded himself into my field of vision.

He disappeared as suddenly as he had appeared.

Oftentimes since have I wondered if the man had been real or some ghostly apparition.

Fiona Parker stood up as I entered her office, my having knocked intrepidly on a sturdy oak door to gain entry. She wore a navy-blue corporate suit with a knee-length skirt and matching tights. She seemed tall but she might have been wearing heels. Her hair was a natural blonde. She was slim and shapely, and her facial features bespoke a no-nonsense efficiency, though they were not entirely without intimations of kindness and fellowship.

After we had introduced ourselves, I accepted her invitation to take a seat.

"Your colleague has been most helpful," I began.

"He's no colleague of mine," the lady retorted, abruptly, like a dog snatching a bone from a hand with its teeth.

"I see," I said, defensively, since the last thing I wanted to do was antagonise her.

"The less you know about that man, the better," she snapped, more a snake spitting venom now than an impatient dog.

Her vituperative tone startled me and made me determined to keep the interview as short as possible. I suspected that the determination was mutual.

The interview proceeded in a peculiar fashion, for it was a sitting standoff, the distance between us more than the two yards or so that was the width of her desk.

I never did find out whether the man who had facilitated the interview had had to resort to playing his card, though there were suggestions in my interlocutor's demeanour that he had.

"I understand that you're looking for Leanne Kenyon."

Hearing her name spoken sent a shiver of anticipation down my spine. I was struggling to contain my emotion. For the first time in my journey to find Leanne, the hope was starting to kill me. I would have taken that scenario at the outset, however, and I calmed myself by telling myself so.

"Yes," I replied, "that is the reason why I'm here."

"Leanne left here a year ago," the lady said. "She went to Fleetpool. She called it 'home'. I know she's from Oxford, so I'm not sure what her connection with Fleetpool is. Anyway, the place obviously means a lot to her."

"Do you know whereabouts in Fleetpool?" I asked. I was unable to believe that I had been unable to find Leanne in several days of searching when she was right under my nose.

"Well, it's not exactly Fleetpool," Ms Parker said. "She came into some money and bought a little café in Sandhills, a few miles up the coast from Fleetpool. The café's called, well, it's called Sandhills Café."

"I know Sandhills," I said gleefully.

That Leanne had come into some money gave me food for thought: if her Uncle Leo were the benefactor then Charles Dickens' tale of Abel Magwitch's financial enrichment of Pip in his novel *Great Expectations* sprang to mind.

"That's where you'll find her."

"I'm supremely grateful." I was running out of ways to express my gratitude.

"I shouldn't be telling you all this, it's more than my job's worth, but you seem to be a decent sort."

Or you were forced to tell me to protect your marriage, I thought to myself, and immediately chided myself for allowing such a grubby notion to occupy my mind for so much as a second.

"One more question," I said. I was hoping that I was not pushing my luck.

"Okay," Fiona sighed as if to convey the message that I was, indeed, pushing my luck.

"Do you happen to know if Leanne had someone special in her life? A boyfriend? A husband even?"

"She said that she had loved only once, and that she would remain faithful to that love by never loving again."

The double-whisky that I ordered at the bar following the interview helped me to get over Fiona's last statement, for its sheer magnitude, and for what it signified, and I spent some time, online, researching Sandhills Café. Even on its official website there was no mention of Leanne. Even there, then, Leanne had no online footprint.

I would drive over to Sandhills at first light the following morning.

Would I sleep like a log that night, knowing that my mission to find Leanne was accomplished, and that the following day we would be together again?

Or would I be so overcome with feverish excitement that sleep would be impossible?

We would be together again.

That statement was both true and false.

False, because we had never been apart.

TWENTY-TWO

Oxford

In the May of 2006, I went to Oxford for a weekend, arriving on the Friday afternoon and returning to Sudbury on the Sunday evening. The weather was fine and warm, and—owing, I suspect, to the fact that it was not a Bank Holiday weekend—there was not an abundance of tourists. The Father of English Literature himself, Geoffrey Chaucer, once said: "Hard is the heart that loveth nought in May." On that weekend, in the city of Matthew Arnold's Dreaming Spires and my Teeming Squires, it was hard, indeed, not to be in love with the world.

My wondrous appreciation of the city of Oxford was accentuated by my state of mind at the time, for I was euphoric, having just graduated from the Open University with a degree in philosophy.

My head was filled with the works comprising the philosophical pantheon (and not just the Western philosophical pantheon either). The word "philosophy" means "lover of wisdom", and that to me was fundamental: the more philosophy in the world, the better, because people who love wisdom enough to pursue it are bound to be good people and so make the world a better place. Not just a *better* place, either, but a *good* place. There we have the essential meaning of Iris Murdoch's *Sovereignty of Good*, her conception of Good founded on Plato's Form of the Good, and acting as the moral foundation of a world separated from the personal god of formal religious belief, with all the moral strictures that come with it.

Iris Murdoch, indeed, was—and remains—a cherished piece of my mental furniture, a gilded throne sitting regally in a once sparse and featureless room.

All philosophers are writers, and some philosophers are great writers *as* philosophers.

Some philosophers are also great writers as *writers*.

Iris Murdoch is one such. She once declared that the aim of literature is to mystify, while the aim of philosophy is to clarify. We might connect Murdoch here with Chekhov, who once quipped that medicine was his wife and literature his mistress. In Iris Murdoch's case, there was no conflict, no duality, only a unity, for she was married as much to mystery as to clarity, an unashamed intellectual bigamist.

All the art and books and music of the entire history of the world was in Oxford, and, in my newfound state of artistic and intellectual fervour, I was desperate to tap into it, to open its ever-opaque bottle and drink thirstily from it.

Oxford was the ideal place for me to spend a few days, alone, exploring, drifting in and out of bookshops and cafés and pubs, immersing myself in the spirit of the place, becoming at one with it, intuiting its *genius loci* and communing with it.

I stayed in a small hotel in Summertown, in North Oxford. I visited all the colleges. I wandered around and through the University Parks, where I watched a couple of hours of a four-day cricket match between the University team and Hampshire and found myself explaining to a group of Japanese tourists that they had not just stumbled upon the enactment of an obscure English fertility rite but were witnessing the national sport in action. I risked ignominy (for people have been known to fall into the River Cherwell) by punting from the Head of the River pub, in Abingdon Road, to the Victoria Arms, in Old Marston, and back.

My Oxford visit had little to do with Leanne. At the time, I was cherishing my memory of her whilst allowing that memory to drift from my consciousness. She was there but fading. She occupied some twilight area of my mind where reality had become so like a dream that I wondered if it had ever been a reality at all. My mind was saying to me: "Leanne might well have been but a dream, so forget her."

She was fading, indeed, but she was still there.

Wherever I went that weekend, I asked somebody, a person at random, if they knew Leanne Kenyon, or knew of her, and was met with one "Sorry, no…" after another. The question was worth asking, and I asked it casually, as if it were of no special moment.

I yielded to the temptation to take a bus to Risinghurst, the Oxford suburb where Leanne had grown up. I did so in a spirit of resignation that I would never see Leanne again. I succeeded with surprising ease in tracking down Robert and Christine Moorhouse, from whom I learned that Leanne had never returned following her departure, and that her Uncle

Leo had moved away (they had no idea where he had gone) about a year before.

Still, seeing with my own eyes the very dwelling where Leanne had spent most of her life had reconnected me with her, somehow, and had served to reinvest her with renewed substance as she began to fade from my recent to my distant past.

Leanne had walked the streets of Oxford, and I am not ashamed to confess that I spent three days worshipping the ground on which she had walked.

How easily the cherishing of somebody's memory first slips into veneration before plunging headlong into idolatry.

Even for a ghost …

TWENTY-THREE

Love

There is no such thing as perfect love, only love, for love is perfect.

There is only love itself.

Love is perfection itself.

Love is perfection.

In the same way, love is beauty.

Love can only ennoble, it cannot corrupt, for if it tends toward corruption then it is not love but a warped negation of love masquerading as love purely for show.

Love is pure virtue with no trace of vice.

It cannot be otherwise.

Love is bound to justice and cannot do what is not just.

Love, then, is beauty and justice and, in each, cannot be other than perfect.

On a par with beauty and justice, love is truth.

Truth is perfect as beauty and justice are perfect.

There is no true love, only truth and love.

For all this to be so, love must come from God, who is Himself love, and who is love Himself.

God is love.

Love is God.

Since the soul proceeds from God—for there can be no soul without God—it follows that love is the love of soul, and that the love of soul is love.

This is love as *agape*. It has no conditions; it does not weigh in the balance; it expects nothing in return; it gives of itself, freely, and mourns not its unrequitedness.

Love is rare.

Love is as rare as a butterfly in a firestorm.

He who loves is but a rarity.

He who talks about love, but does not love, is as common as the man who loves is rare.

He talks the talk of love but cannot walk the walk.

He who loves the soul of one loves the soul of all.

He who finds God finds love.

He who finds love finds the soul.

One might first find the soul, which leads to love, which leads to God.

Or one might first find God and, through love, reach the soul.

It is all for one and one for all.

Convince me that there is no God, and I will renounce neither love nor the soul.

Rather, I will dedicate both to the God that might have been.

TWENTY-FOUR

Essence

La Belle Noiseuse (*The Beautiful Troublemaker*) is a four-hour cinematic epic directed by Jacques Rivette, one of the finest filmmakers to emerge from La Nouvelle Vague (the French New Wave), which began to take shape towards the end of the nineteen-fifties.

In this 1991 work, Rivette crafts an emotionally charged masterpiece in which what happens beneath the surface is key.

The film describes how a retired artist is persuaded to produce one last painting, an invitation that he might well have declined had the prospective model not been a beautiful young woman.

Edouard Frenhofer (played by Michel Piccoli) is the ageing painter in question. He lives in an isolated chateau in the south of France with his much younger wife Liz (Jane Burkin).

Porbus (Gilles Arbona) is an art-dealer with a plan: to introduce rookie artist Nicolas (David Bursztein) and his exquisite girlfriend, Marianne (Emmanuelle Béart), to Frenhofer with a view to persuading him to complete a work begun ten years before, but unaccountably shelved, a study of the female form and character using Liz as his model.

Porbus, then, sees an opportunity and duly seizes it when he suggests that Marianne (who, in turn, is much younger than Liz) be the impetus to finish the painting, the idea being that her youth and beauty could not fail to stimulate Frenhofer's fading powers back into life and so endow him with one last acclaimed work for posterity.

Frenhofer agrees to do the painting, and Nicolas consents on behalf of Marianne.

Though Marianne is indignant about the agreement's having been made without her consent, she is intrigued enough eventually to submit herself to the painter's scrutiny and present herself at the chateau the following day.

In the studio, artist and model spar almost wordlessly. Marianne becomes possessed by her own alluringness and bewitching power, even as she resents Frenhofer for capturing it, for she knows that in capturing these qualities, which flow from her outer beauty, he is distilling her very soul.

The viewer senses that Marianne anticipates the outcome: that Frenhofer, moved more by the urge to capture his model's essence than her outer beauty, will produce something so shocking that she will recoil from it in horror, as the sight of her essential self peering back at her—a grotesque self-revelation in mirror-like reflection—proves too much for her to bear.

For the sake of putting on a show, Frenhofer hides the portrait—he puts it out of reach in a vault—and hurriedly paints an alternative, more commonplace version of Marianne.

Porbus declares the painting a success and a celebratory party is held.

After the party, Nicolas and Marianne (who has been changed profoundly by her encounter with the artist and with herself) go their separate ways.

The Beautiful Troublemaker is the name of Frenhofer's unfinished portrait of his wife, Liz, to aid the completion of which Marianne was engaged as Frenhofer's muse.

Of course, the real Beautiful Troublemaker is the woman who has taken Liz's place as the artist's model and inspiration, the woman who is now roughly Liz's age when her husband began painting her.

Is Leanne my Beautiful Troublemaker? She is. But only in the sense that, like Frenhofer with Marianne, I painted her essence. For that there was no pen and wash, no sketches, no multiple arrangements and adjustments of the model's pose in the studio, no battle of wills, no mutual resentment, antipathy, and suspicion.

It was done entirely from memory.

It was accomplished, indeed, by my communing with Leanne's soul.

Upon seeing the painting, Leanne would not recoil from it. Far from it …

Of that I was certain.

TWENTY-FIVE

Consummation

Consummatum est, indeed, I thought to myself as I looked down from my vantage point in the carpark behind Sandhills Café, which nestled cosily in a gorgeously secluded spot on the curve of a small bay facing west towards the Irish Sea.

The day was warm and sunny enough for me to survey the scene from behind sunglasses and with the car window more than halfway down.

Consummation was mine. I had fought the good fight and won. It was over.

I had gone to bed early, slept well, and stopped en route to Sandhills at the Marine Gardens Hotel, where I apologised to Nadine for not returning the day before and agreed to collect her that Monday evening and take her to Norwich.

I had caught her at the hotel by chance, since she was there only because she was saying goodbye to her former colleagues. She had planned to travel to Norwich by train. I had saved her the trouble. I would be glad of the company; and she would prove to be delightful company, a young woman full of amusing stories and brimming with ideas for the future, mature beyond her years.

I looked at my watch. The time was eleven-twenty-three, too late for breakfast and too early for lunch, but the café was still busy with people eating and drinking on the expansive terrace overlooking the golden, sandy beach.

Nervously, expectantly, I waited for a forty-year-old woman to appear on the terrace.

Then she came.

She danced elegantly around the tables like a ballerina—she was all grace and poise—bringing drinks on a tray and taking away empty glasses, turning a mundane task into an artform.

It was Leanne. It was her shape, her movement, her aura.

Only the clothes were different: she had put away childish things and taken up the things of a woman.

She was a woman of distinction now in violet-coloured skirt, sky-blue blouse, and black boots.

Her hair was shoulder-length and black as ever it had been.

"That's my girl." I could not help but utter these words to myself about the woman.

Having fetched the packaged painting from the boot of the car, I descended to the steps of the café entrance and peered inside. There she was, washing plates and glasses, busily, her back to me, about to meet her known destiny.

Tears fell pitilessly from my eyes.

I stepped towards the bar.

She was engrossed in her work.

She stopped working but did not turn around immediately; for a few seconds, she prepared herself for what she knew she would see, for *whom* she knew she would see, having sensed his presence behind her in a moment that she knew was fated.

Eventually, she turned around. She put her hands to her face and, as I had done, smiled tears.

We were separated by the width of the bar. For a moment, which we both saw as comical, we were unsure where we would come together, my side or hers.

For the sake of a modicum of privacy, we chose the relative seclusion of Leanne's side of the bar. I went to her. I placed the painting, still in its packaging, on the bar.

"Is that for me?" she asked, her tender voice churning my soul.

"It *is* you," I replied.

Somehow, she understood.

"Happy birthday," I said.

"Happy birthday," she said back.

We were soulmates who would echo each other's words for all eternity.

We were nothing less than that.

We held each other as if we would never let go.

"I knew you would come," she wept. "I just knew it."

She was the same Leanne: yesterday, today, and forever.